Chromium Cauldron

By: Terri Talley Venters

An Elements Of Mystery Book

Editor: Leslie S. Talley

Print ISBN-13:978-1979249423

eBook ISBN-10:1979249423

Smashwords ISBN-9781370491339

If you are interested in purchasing more works of this nature, please stop by www.ElementsOfMystery.com.
Printed in The United States of America

Manchester Family Tree
New Orleans Coven
Modern Day

Olivia Manchester—Bartholomew Manchester

Violet Manchester—Toliver Waynesfield *m. 1905*   *(Cobalt Cauldron)*

Beatrice Manchester—Prince Peter *m. 1922*   *(Chromium Cauldron)*
b. 1906

Daphne Manchester—Peter Manchester

Penelope Manchester—St. Michael the Archangel   *(Copper Cauldron)*

Catherine (Cat) Manchester *twins* Conner Manchester   *(Zirconium Cauldron)*

Elements of Mystery Books
By:
Terri Talley Venters

Prologue

Zeus perched upon the edge of Mount Olympus, studying the mortals on Earth. Jealous of their opulent lifestyle and vast wealth. Rage consumed him. *They live better than the Gods!*

"You summoned me, your Majesty?" Poseidon bowed holding his prized Trident.

"Yes, I'd like to show you something." Zeus gestured to the edge of the clouds where they could spy on the mortals below.

"Oh my, the mortals live better than us. At least the rich ones do." Poseidon shook his head in frustration.

"We must do something. I can't bear to watch them so happy and prosperous. They've forgotten us and never make us any offerings or prayers. They now pray to Jesus or Allah. I thought we'd taught them a lesson when you sank Atlantis. But now the lost city is mostly forgotten by the mortals. They think it's a myth, not a catastrophe caused by the angry Gods."

"What did you have in mind this time?" Poseidon asked.

"I've heard about this new ship the mortals built. It's the most luxurious ocean liner ever made. Many of the wealthy have booked passage for the maiden voyage from Southampton, England to New York City," Zeus explained. He studied the model globe and traced the ship's planned route.

"Ah, yes. I've heard of it. They claim it's unsinkable." Poseidon nodded.

"That's what angers me the most. I heard the mortals boast that 'not even the Gods could sink the Titanic.'"

1

Chapter One

December 31, 1911
Manchester Mansion
New Orleans

"Grandpa, can you please read me a bedtime story?" Bea, short for Beatrice Manchester, asked her doting grandfather, Bart. Her five-year-old body lay in her pink bedroom. Her long, black hair fanned across a pink pillowcase. The bedroom was once her mother's room before she married her father, Toliver, the reincarnated spirit of Tutankhamun, Pharaoh of Ancient Egypt.

"Of course, my dear. Since your parents are out celebrating the new year, I'd love to read you a story." Bart sat in the wing-back chair next to Bea's bed. His long, blond hair was tied back in a ponytail with a black, silk ribbon. He stared at Bea with matching magical eyes—one blue and one green.

"Can I have a kitty, Grandpa?" Bea begged.

"Well, of course you can, my dear. But let's wait until we get back from Florida," Bart promised.

"Why are we going to Florida for so long?" Bea pulled the covers up to her chin to ward off the chill from the cold December evening.

"We're staying for the Winter Season. But this time, instead of staying at the Ponce De Leon Hotel in St. Augustine, we're going to stay at Henry Flagler's winter home in Palm Beach."

"How big is his home?" Bea asked, curious about the wealthy railroad tycoon.

"It's over one-hundred-thousand square feet. Ten times larger than our Manchester Mansion." Bart waved his arm around her room.

"Whoa! I guess he has plenty of room for all of us. Are Daddy's parents coming, too?" Bea referred to her paternal grandparents, Isaac and Manon Waynesfield.

"Yes. In fact, it's because of Isaac that we are staying at Whitehall. Henry uses Isaac's new bank in Palm Beach. There are a lot of wealthy Americans who winter in Florida," Grandpa explained.

"Okay, I guess it makes sense to wait until we get back to adopt my kitten. I wouldn't want to leave him or her all alone in this big house," she rationalized.

"You are very wise for one so young," he praised.

"When will I get my powers, Grandpa?" Bea crossed her arms and pouted.

"I'm sure it will be very soon. You'll grow up to be a beautiful and powerful witch like your mother, my daughter, Violet."

"But didn't Mommy get her powers when she was six? When she found King Tut's tomb in Egypt?" Bea recalled the story of how her parents found one another in this life with the help of the Cobalt Cauldron.

"Well, we thought she got her first power when she was six because she had a vision which led us to the tomb. But it wasn't really her vision. It was Toliver using the Cobalt Cauldron spell to fill her mind with visions. She didn't get her real power of foresight until she was older." Grandpa Bart held Bea's hand.

"Oh, well that makes me feel better for not having any powers yet." Bea smiled.

"Speaking of powers, I thought I'd read you a story from the *Book of Cauldrons*."

"Can we read it in the attic? I like going up there at night because it's spooky." Bea grinned devilishly.

"You're are the most fearless witch I have ever known. Yes, let's go to the attic. I assume you wish to ride on my shoulders." He knelt next to the bed.

Nodding eagerly, Bea climbed on Grandpa's shoulders and placed her hands gently on his neck.

Grandpa Bart stood, and his knees cracked. "Ahh, pretty soon you'll be too big to carry on my shoulders." He carried Bea up two flights of wooden stairs to the attic. He retrieved the large brass key from his pocket and unlocked the door. After entering the dark attic, he knelt down in front of the fireplace.

Bea climbed off Grandpa and rubbed her arms to ward off the chill. Wiggling her tiny fingers at the fireplace, she envisioned orange flames roaring to life. The fire started, and Bea gasped.

"Grandpa, I just got my first power!"

Chapter Two

"How wonderful, my dear! Your first power, and I was here to witness it. Your parents will be sad that they missed it. It's a very important rite of passage for witches and wizards," Grandpa explained.

Beaming, Bea studied the various volumes of books shelved next to the fireplace. Running her tiny fingers across the various spines, she named a few of the books—*Book of Spells, Book of Demons, Book of Angels, Book of Trolls and Giants, Book of Monsters, Book of Legends, Book of Fairies, Book of Gods and Goddesses,* and *Book of Cauldrons.* "Ah, here it is." Bea pulled the enormous volume from the shelf. Its weight strained her.

"Here. Allow me." Bart grabbed the volume and sat on one of the wing-back chairs in front of the fireplace.

Bea climbed onto his lap and rested the back of her head against his shoulder.

"Where would you like to start, my dear?" Grandpa asked.

Placing her index finger on her dimpled cheek, she said, "Something new and interesting. Something about a cauldron that we don't have."

"Ah, excellent idea, my dear. You probably know about all the ones we have—Copper, Cobalt, Jade, Onyx, Iron, Lead, etc." He flipped the pages.

"Oh, what's that one? Is it silver?" Bea asked, pointing to the open page of the *Book of Cauldrons.* The large silver cauldron was the most beautiful and ornate cauldron she'd ever seen. It was enormous and even had handles.

"Not silver, silver tarnishes which changes the property of the metal. This is the Chromium

Cauldron. And yes, it is the biggest and most ornate cauldron there is."

"Have you seen it Grandpa?" Bea gazed at the picture of the cauldron meticulously painted in the *Book of Cauldrons.*

"No, I haven't. But I recall our ancestor, Mordecai Manchester, receiving a Chromium Cauldron from his true love."

"Really?" Bea flipped the page to reveal a colorful painting of a mermaid.

Bart read the carefully scribed words in the book, "It says that the Chromium Cauldron is very rare."

"What's its power?" Bea asked.

He continued reading, "The Chromium Cauldron allows humans to breathe underwater. By making a potion with sea water and dragon shrooms, a human can drink from the Chromium Cauldron and be able to breathe underwater."

"Where does one find a Chromium Cauldron? And why is there a painting of a mermaid?" Bea asked.

"You need to study Latin, my dear. Then you'd be able to read for yourself," Grandpa criticized.

"I will take Latin more seriously, now. I want to read all of these books. Why doesn't someone translate these books into English? We live in America, after all." Bea crossed her arms and pouted. She wasn't lazy, but Latin was a hard language to learn, and she only recently began reading and writing in English.

"Since Latin is now a dead language, very few people know how to read and write it. Keeping the books in Latin secures their contents. We wouldn't want nonmagical humans to learn all about us," he explained.

"But where are all the Chromium Cauldrons?"

"The mermaids have them. They hid them in the ocean. They don't want humans to find them and use them to breathe underwater and destroy their aquatic homes."

"How can humans use a Chromium Cauldron if the mermaids hid them all?" Bea asked.

"Ah, on rare occasions, a mermaid or merman swims to the surface and falls in love with a human. Then the mermaid presents their true love with a Chromium Cauldron so they can breathe underwater. But over time, the mermaids have forgotten the potion ingredients which are required for the Chromium Cauldron spell."

"But a witch?"

"Ah, you are very bright, Baby Bea. Yes, if a mermaid or merman falls in love with a wizard or witch, the witch can mix the correct potion for the Chromium Cauldron spell."

"Where is their home?" Bea asked.

"Good question." Grandpa Bart ran his index finger along the Latin words. "It references the *Book of Legends*."

Bea jumped off his lap and searched the bookshelf. "There it is, Grandpa."

He returned the *Book of Cauldrons* and removed the *Book of Legends*.

The pair resumed their positions in the chair in front of the fire and flipped the pages of the enormous *Book of Legends.*

They stopped on the colorful painting of mermaids in their palatial home under the sea.

"It's beautiful." Bea ran her fingers over the golden palace.

Bart studied the text. "Interesting. I don't think I ever knew this part of the legend."

"What is it Grandpa? What is this place?" Bea studied the beautiful mermaids.

"The city was once on the surface. It was a lush and beautiful island with modern technology. The Gods grew jealous of this advanced civilization. So jealous that they sank the island with an enormous earthquake and covered it with a tidal wave. The mermaids found it in the ocean and moved in."

"What is the city called?" Bea asked.

"Atlantis."

Chapter Three

"Why couldn't we *Eo Ire Itum* here?" Bea asked, referring to the instantaneous travel method available to witches and wizards, named for the Latin word, 'to travel'. She sat in the horse-drawn carriage with her family. They took the long train ride from New Orleans to Jacksonville, then from Jacksonville to Palm Beach with stops in St. Augustine and Ormond Beach. Now they approached Henry and Mary Flagler's winter home—Whitehall.

"Didn't you like the train ride?" Toliver, her father, sat next to Bea on one side while Violet, her mother, sat on the other. Her grandparents, Bart, Olivia, Isaac, and Manon rode in the carriage behind them.

"It was fun at first, but then it got booorrring." Bea whined.

"Well, we're almost there, my dear. But I promise that we'll *Eo Ire Itum* home at the end of the season." The horses turned onto a dirt road lined on both sides with beautiful palm trees that nearly reached the sky.

"Whoa!" Mommy pointed to the enormous white mansion with black shutters and huge Greek columns supporting the two-story veranda.

"It's beautiful." Mommy turned to Daddy and asked. "How did we get invited here?"

"Through my father and our banking empire. Henry Flagler is our biggest client at the bank. In fact, my father opened a branch in Palm Beach just for Henry," Daddy explained.

"Are we staying here, Daddy? Or at the hotel?" Bea asked.

"We're staying here. Most guests stay at the Royal Poinciana Hotel. And if that's full, they stay at the nearby Breakers. They are both right on the beach.

But since Henry and Grandpa Isaac are such good friends, Henry invited us all to stay in his mansion."

The carriage circled around and stopped in front of Whitehall.

"How many rooms does this mansion have if he can accommodate all seven of us for three months?" Bea stepped out of the carriage and gawked at the enormous white columns.

Isaac stepped out of the other carriage and said, "Seventy-five rooms. Henry built the mansion as a wedding present for his third wife, Mary Lily Kenan Flagler."

"Three wives?" Bea asked, shocked that someone got married three times.

"Long story. His first wife, also named Mary, died in childbirth. Then his second wife, Alice, went crazy. Henry divorced her, then moved her to a loony bin in New York," Isaac explained.

"Isaac Waynesfield!" Grandma Manon slapped Grandpa Isaacs's hand.

"Sorry, insane asylum," he corrected.

"How much did this house cost, Grandpa Isaac?" Bea inherited Daddy's and Grandpa Isaacs's knack for numbers.

"Beatrice Manchester. It is rude to ask how much someone's house cost, how much money they make, or how old they are," Mommy scolded.

"Oh, I thought I just couldn't ask Mr. Flagler directly." Bea dropped her chin.

"It's all right, my dear. You're just curious about numbers. Henry built this house in 1905. It cost $2,500,000 to build and $1,500,000 to furnish and decorate."

Bea quickly did the sum. "Four million dollars?"

A butler, with a stiff posture and grim expression, opened the enormous double doors of Whitehall.

Bea grabbed one hand of both grandpas and walked through the open doors. A cold breeze blew from the ocean, chilling Bea.

The foyer was enormous—two stories tall. A double staircase dominated the center with wrought-iron handrails and polished white marble. At the base of the staircase sat a man and a woman in matching green chairs. The man was really old, and the lady was half his age. *His daughter?*

"Isaac, you're back." The old man, presumably Mr. Flagler, stood and smiled with open arms.

Isaac embraced his longtime friend and biggest banking client. "Henry, it's great to see you again. Thank you for inviting my family to your lovely home."

"It's the least I could do after withdrawing millions from your bank to build this." Henry waved his arm around his palatial winter home. "You remember my lovely wife, Mary."

His wife? Why was she so much younger? She must've married him for his fortune.

Mary stood regally and extended her gloved hand. Grandpa Isaac kissed it.

"Mary, beautiful as ever." Isaac kissed Mary Flagler's gloved hand.

Everyone else greeted their host and hostess.

Henry knelt in front of Bea. "Ahh, this must be Beatrice. Your grandfather talks about you all the time. I thought he exaggerated about your beauty. But now I see that he did not. You really do have the most beautiful eyes, like your mother and Manon—one blue and one green."

"Thank you very much, Mr. Flagler, Mrs. Flagler. You have a lovely home. Thank you for letting us stay here." Bea curtsied.

"Ah, what impeccable manners you have, my dear." Mary kissed Bea's cheeks. "I know just the perfect room for you, it's pink."

Bea beamed and clapped her hands excitedly.

"Yes, thank you for letting us all stay in your beautiful home instead of the hotel. Not that the Royal Poinciana and the Breakers aren't magnificent, but you honor us with your generous hospitality." Isaac bowed.

"Nonsense, you're family. I remember when Violet and Toliver honeymooned at the Ponce De Leon Hotel in St. Augustine," Henry boasted.

"Bea was born nine months later." Daddy winked and squeezed Mommy's hand.

"Besides, bookings are down this season. Many of our friends decided to winter in Europe and take that new monstrosity of a ship back to New York," Henry explained.

"Ah, yes, the Titanic," Isaac said.

Chapter Four

Bea followed the entourage up the marble staircase to the second floor. The walls were beautifully decorated with paintings and portraits. A long corridor appeared with dozens of doors, each leading to a bedroom.

"This is where you'll spend the next three months." Mary escorted Bea into an enormous pink bedroom. A white onyx fireplace warmed the room on this chilly January afternoon. Near the fireplace was a mirrored make-up table filled with perfume and hair paraphernalia. To the right was a meticulously made bed with pink satin pillows and blankets. Pink curtains hung above the head board providing a canopy.

Bea walked to the large window on the opposite side of the room. She stared in awe at the blue ocean.

"Mommy, the ocean!" Bea pointed. "Can I go?"

"Of course, dear. But let's settle in first, we have a lot of unpacking to do," Mommy said.

"The servants can unpack for you. Go ahead and see the beautiful beach. Don't forget a parasol to protect your beautiful skin from the sun." Mary smiled.

"Okay, be careful. Don't swim in the water by yourself. One, it's freezing cold, and two, I don't want you to drown. And be back before dark," Mommy warned.

"Yippee!" Bea hugged her parents.

"Violet, Toliver, your room is next door." Mary gestured to a door adjoining the two rooms.

Mommy and Daddy followed Mary into the green room next door. "Have fun and be safe." Mommy waved.

Once her parents left, Bea ran to the large pink bed and jumped on it. She didn't even come close to hitting the ceiling of the tall room.

"No jumping on the bed!" Mommy hollered from the next room.

How did she know? Sighing, Bea slumped. A shiny object caught her attention, literally. Bea walked to the dressing table and sat on the pink cushioned chair. Sitting up straight like a proper lady, she studied her reflection in the mirror. Grabbing the heavy, silver hairbrush, she admired its intricate carvings on the back. She brushed her long, black locks until her hair shone beautifully.

Bea picked up the glass bottle of perfume. Holding the bottle in one hand and the rubber ball attached to the bottle's tube in the other, Bea sprayed the pungent fragrance. Feeling sophisticated, she admired her reflection in the mirror.

She was pretty, at least her parents thought so. But she wondered how she would look when she grew up. Probably just like her mother, she presumed. Then she wondered who she would marry and what he would look like. *Would he have dark hair like her Daddy, or blond hair like Grandpa Bart?*

Satisfied with her appearance, Bea walked to the window and gazed at the open sea. Its vastness made her feel as if her life was full of endless possibilities. Thinking of the ocean and wondering about her future husband, her mind recalled the tale from the *Book of Cauldrons*—the Chromium Cauldron. The cauldrons were in the ocean, protected by mermaids. *But where?* And a mermaid may present a human with a Chromium Cauldron if they were their one true love. Thinking of mermaids, true loves, and the Chromium Cauldron, Bea was magically beckoned to the ocean.

Chapter Five

Grabbing her violet parasol and a towel, Bea slowly walked downstairs like a lady. She passed through the beautifully appointed two-story foyer which served as a receiving room, then crossed through gigantic front doors. The creepy butler bowed as she crossed the threshold, closing the door behind her. Once outside, Bea couldn't run to the ocean fast enough.

Passing the same rows of palm trees when she arrived at Whitehall, she longed to climb them. *But how?* Without branches, she'd have to hug the tree to pull herself up. Shaking her head, she let the distraction go and vowed to find more suitable trees to climb later.

After passing the palm trees, Violet crossed a dirt road. Another long row of trees lined another dirt path. The cypress trees were tall and skinny, too. But unlike the palm trees, the cypress ones were full of branches, begging to be climbed.

With ease, she climbed the tallest tree to the tippy top and was rewarded with a breathtaking view. Bea admired the beautiful Royal Poinciana Hotel to the left. The Breakers was between her and the ocean. The view on the right was miles of sandy beaches with a few homes scattered along the shore line.

Turning back towards Whitehall, Bea admired the beautiful mansion from this vantage point. Behind Whitehall flowed a waterway. Boats were moored on wooden docks along the waterway. The thought of a sailboat ride with her parents made her glad that she'd spend the next three months here.

The ocean beckoned her, and she turned and gazed at the open water. Sunbathers stood on the beach near tents. They seemed to be packing up for the day. It was nearing tea time after all. The Breakers' guests walked back to the hotel. The beach cleared out quickly, and Bea enjoyed the view from her vantage point.

Something jumped in the ocean. *A dolphin or a porpoise?* Sharks wouldn't jump like that. It jumped again, this time doing a twist in the air. Singing echoed from the creature, like it was glad humans no longer cluttered the beach. On the third jump, Bea got a better look at this creature. The bottom half was the long tail of a scaly fish, but the top half.... Bea had to blink because she thought her eyes played tricks on her. The top half was pale and looked like a human with arms and a head.

A mermaid?

Bea scurried down the tree, then ran to the beach as fast as her tiny legs allowed. Although sore from tree climbing, she didn't let that hinder her sprint to the ocean. She came to the lobby of the Breakers. Focusing her efforts to not get distracted by shiny objects, she ran past the bellhops, through the lobby, and straight out the back of the hotel to the beach.

"Miss? You can't run in here. Where are your parents?" a man in a beige suit hollered.

Ignoring the protest, Bea ran onto the sandy beach and stared at the ocean. She scanned the water where she *thought* she saw a mermaid just a few minutes ago. But nothing but crashing waves occupied the spot.

Sitting on the sandy beach, she unlaced her shoes, then stepped into the cold water of the ocean. "Brrrr." Covering her arms to ward off the chill of the freezing water, she halted her immersion into the ocean.

Sighing with disappointment, she scanned the water along the shore. The last of the Breakers' guests vacated the beach. A pile of boulders lined part of the shoreline, jettying out into the Atlantic. Bea climbed the boulders skillfully, and walked out to the furthest point. From this vantage point, Bea admired the ocean and its crashing waves.

Something jumped out of the water and flipped in the air, making a large splash as the aquatic creature reentered the water. Bea glimpsed the tail of whatever splashed back into the water.

Something moved near her feet, just where the water crashed onto the rocks. Something shined beneath the surface. A blond head submerged underwater. It was a boy! *Or was it?*

Bea knelt on the rock to get closer to the blond hair floating just beneath the surface. The sun broke through the clouds and shined on the water below. Attached to the blond hair, was the face of a boy.

Was he drowning? Should she jump in and save him? But when he smiled at her, she knew he wasn't drowning. A large fish tail rose out of the water and splashed back down on the surface. Salt water sprayed Bea's face and stung her eyes. The boy giggled and swam away. But a few yards away, he jumped out of the water and flipped into the air.

From this close range, Bea was rewarded with a great view of this magnificent creature. He was a little bigger than her, but not much. His upper half was a human boy with blond hair. Arms extended from his shoulders as he flipped back down into the water. A large tail, like a dolphin's but with scales, shimmered with a teal hue.

He swam out to sea, performing more flips along the way. He was definitely a young merman.

Chapter Six

Incredulous, Bea stared at the water where the young merman last splashed down into the water. Praying she'd see him again, she waited for over an hour.

"Baby Bea? Is that you?" a voice hollered from the shore.

Turning, the setting sun shone in her eyes. Squinting, she recognized the voice which echoed from the shadowed figure on the beach. "Grandpa?"

"Hello, Bea. I worried about you. You missed tea time." Grandpa Bart walked towards the rocks, but stopped at the first boulder.

"Sorry, Grandpa. Don't come up on the rocks. I'll climb down to you." Bea skillfully traversed the rocks back to shore.

"Thank you, my dear. I'm afraid me and my old bones might slip on the rocks and fall. I'd hate to break something on our first day here." Grandpa held out his hand to guide Bea down the last boulder and onto the sandy beach.

"Can we collect sea shells?" Bea asked.

"Of course, we can." He held out his hand, she took it, and they walked along the sandy seashore.

Crabs with glowing eyes scurried sideways, then disappeared into their holes in the sand. Sandpipers ran out with the tide and poked their beaks into the wet sand where bubbles formed from periwinkles. The birds pulled out the shells, scurried back to the sand as the tide came in, and pecked open their slimy feasts awaiting in the now open shells.

Bea stopped in front of a sand dollar, knelt, then gently picked up the fragile shell. "Look, Grandpa. It's all in one piece."

"Exquisite, my dear. How many shells have you collected this afternoon?" He led her south along the shore.

"This is my first one." Guilt consumed her, and she dropped her head.

"What have you been doing all this time?" he asked.

Kicking the sand, she contemplated whether or not to tell Grandpa about the young merman. She could hardly believe it herself, let alone expect others to believe her tale.

"Well, first there were these enormous cypress trees on the way here."

"Let me guess, you climbed the tallest one." He grinned.

"I had to. The view from the top was amazing. At first, there were a lot of people on the beach, but by the time I climbed down and ran out here, everyone was gone."

"Tea time, can't miss that." Grandpa rubbed his belly, obviously satisfied with the tiny sandwiches and tasty sweets which accompanied tea. "You missed a great one. The cream-filled scones were the best I ever tasted. Everything is top notch at Whitehall."

"Then I climbed on those rocks and watched the ocean." Bea waved her arm back to the rocks.

"Did you see anything interesting?" he asked.

"Well, I did see something jump out of the water and splash back down several times."

"Probably a porpoise or a dolphin. They're magnificent creatures," Grandpa said.

"That's what I thought at first, too. Something jumped in the water when I was up in the tree. That was an amazing view from up there. I could see Whitehall, the Breakers, Royal Poinciana, and the ocean."

"This place is spectacular. But what do you mean, that's what you thought *at first*?" he asked.

Nothing got past Grandpa.

"Well, I saw...you're never going to believe me." Bea dropped her chin and kicked the sand beneath her feet.

"What did you see? Tell me, my dear," he pleaded.

"I saw a young merman!"

Chapter Seven

"Why can't I eat dinner with the grown-ups?" Bea asked, wearing her new, pink dress which matched her pink room at Whitehall. Her new shoes, called Mary Janes, were shiny, but uncomfortable. She longed to kick them off and walk in the sand by the ocean and talk to the young merman.

"Because you'll be *bored* to death listening to grown-ups talking about grown-up stuff. You'll have much more fun eating dinner with the other children in the music room. They have a piano and a harp. You can play games after you eat dinner," Violet explained.

"There are other children here? How old are they? What are their names? Where are they from?" Bea fired her questions in rapid succession. She walked down the grand staircase with her parents. They arrived in the grand foyer with the large green thrones.

"I have no idea, my dear." Daddy squeezed her hand. "You'll have to ask them yourself."

"I like your dress, Mommy. It's the same color as your name—Violet." Bea admired her beautiful mother.

"Thank you, Bea. I wore this dress when I met your father. It's old, but one can't wear the same dress twice during the season. I'm just glad I can still fit into it after having you." Mommy held Bea's other hand.

"The best day of my life, except for our wedding day and when you were born, of course." Daddy beamed at Mommy. There were still in love after seven years of marriage. But that wasn't surprising, they were soul mates, after all. Daddy was the reincarnated spirit of Tutankhamen, and Mommy was the reincarnated spirit of her ancestor, Cordelia Garrison Manchester.

"Toliver, Violet, how wonderful to see you again." A man kissed Violet's cheek, then shook Toliver's hand.

"George Washington Vanderbilt, how wonderful to see you, too. It's been years. How are you? I've heard about your place in North Carolina." Toliver grabbed two glasses of champagne from a tray. He handed one to Violet, then raised his glass and toasted, "To the Flaglers for having us in their beautiful home."

"Here, here." The grown-ups toasted.

"I am fantastic. And yes, I've built a hunting lodge in the beautiful Blue Ridge Mountains. I named it Biltmore. You'll have to come and stay, just not in the winter because it's too cold. I like to winter in Florida with the rest of the *ton*."

"You're being modest, as usual, George. I hear the Biltmore is even bigger than Whitehall," Daddy whispered.

"Well, what do we have here? You look about the same age as my nephew." The old man knelt in front of Bea.

"Forgive me, Beatrice, this is Mr. Vanderbilt." Daddy introduced them.

Bea curtsied. "It's nice to meet you, sir. I'm five-years-old."

"Ah, perfect for my nephew. He's six. Perhaps when you're older, he can court you." Mr. Vanderbilt winked at Daddy.

"Daddy, what does *court* mean? Like the kind of court with a judge? Or the kind of court in a palace?"

"I'll explain when you're older. I'm not ready to think about my baby girl being courted by anyone." Daddy grimaced.

"Ah, there he is. Cornelius, come meet the spellbinding Beatrice Manchester," Mr. Vanderbilt said, ignorant of the irony.

22

Cornelius, while picking his nose, walked towards the group. He had black hair and wore a suit, but with knickers instead of long pants like the grown-ups. His face was hideous, and his teeth crooked.

But Bea remembered her manners and curtsied like a well-bred young lady. "It's nice to meet you, Master Vanderbilt."

"Wow, you're pretty." Cornelius smiled, obviously trying to do so without revealing his crooked teeth.

Repulsed by this boy, Bea thought of her young blond merman in the Atlantic. She couldn't wait to see the magnificent, magical creature again.

Chapter Eight

"Daddy, look, there's a pretty girl about my age." A beautiful blonde girl pointed at Bea.

Bea turned to the girl who dragged her father to the group.

"JP, great to see you." Toliver shook JP's hand.

"My business rival. But more than your banks, I envy you for your beautiful wife with exquisite eyes." JP turned to Violet and bowed.

While the parents chit chatted, Bea and the blonde girl studied each other intensely.

Being the sweet little girl, Bea smiled and said, "Hello, I'm Bea. What's your name?"

The blonde girl, with the most beautiful cerulean blue eyes, wore her golden hair in perfect curls. A big lavender bow in her hair matched her lavender silk dress with white lace. Without smiling, she said, "Hello, my name is Shirley."

Something wasn't right about this girl, but Bea couldn't decipher what was wrong with her. Most little girls her age smiled at one another, then became fast best friends. At least that's how it worked with her Manchester cousins.

"Oh, good, our daughters met," JP said to Toliver.

"Cornelius, come and meet the lovely Shirley Morgan, she's about your age." Mr. Vanderbilt gestured.

Now Shirley smiled with the sweetest expression. She curtsied to Cornelius, then held out her gloved hand for him to kiss. "It's nice to meet you, Master Vanderbilt."

Cornelius didn't know what to do with Shirley's hand. "Uh, er. It's nice to meet you, too, Miss Morgan." He awkwardly rotated her hand, but instead of kissing it, he shook it.

Mary Flagler glided across the marble foyer wearing an elegant ivory gown. A gorgeous necklace adorned her neck. She leaned over to them and said, "Children, you may now go into the music room. Your dinner will be served there shortly."

Bea studied her parents for guidance.

"Go ahead, my dear. Make some friends. We'll see you in the morning." Daddy touched his hand to her cheek.

"But not too, early. We probably won't get back to our room until dawn." Mommy grinned, then winked at Daddy.

Cornelius ran into the music room. Several other boys his age sprinted after him, obviously starving.

"Cornelius, ladies first," Mr. Vanderbilt scolded.

The boys halted in front of the music room to allow the young ladies to enter first.

Shirley sauntered to the music room. Holding her chin up high and her shoulders back, she entered the opulent music room with an air of snobbery.

Why is Shirley acting so weird? And why is she so nice to the boys, but not to the girls? Bea wondered. She never really had any friends back home in New Orleans. She didn't go to school with the other children in the Garden District. Her parents explained that the schoolhouse didn't teach what she needed to learn—Latin, Gaelic, German, and the *Books of Spells, Legends, and Cauldrons.*

Bea wondered if something was wrong with her. Since she spent most of her time with other witches and wizards, she took it for granted that her magical eyes were accepted. But apparently, non-magical folks considered her a freak.

Cornelius waved at a table in the music room. "Oh, Miss Manchester. Would you like to sit next to me?"

Shirley shot Bea a hateful stare. "Stay away from Master Vanderbilt, he's mine!"

Fine, you can have him. I'm destined for my merman.

Chapter Nine

All yours? You can have that ugly, nose-pickin'
brat. Bea thought.

The focal point of the music room was a beautiful,
white onyx fireplace. A grand piano, to the left of the
fireplace, beckoned to be played. In the right corner, a
gold harp boasted long, golden strings. The green and
white walls provided a light, airy feel. Electric lamps
illuminated the room with intricately decorated lamp
shades to subdue the bright lights that electricity
provided.

Several gaming tables were intimately placed
throughout the room. They were set with china and
silverware. But after dinner, various games could be
played—cards, carriage, chess, and checkers.

Shirley snuck in and sat in the seat Cornelius
offered to Bea. Her aura was bitter and jealous. She
sat ramrod straight with her shoulders back. Turning
triumphantly to Bea, she stuck out her tongue

Cornelius shrugged, obviously not caring which
pretty, wealthy girl from an affluent family sat next to
him.

Taking the seat furthest away from Cornelius and
Shirley, relief swept through Bea. *Thank God, I'm not*
sitting   next   to   these   awful   children. But
unfortunately, she was still at the same table since this
was the only table the servants set for the children's
dinner.

"I'm starving. These servants are so slow. I wonder
what's for dinner. I hope it's good enough for me. I
only eat gourmet meals either prepared by our French
chef, or at one of the finest restaurants in New York,"
Shirley bragged.

"I don't care what we eat, I'm starved." Cornelius
slumped in his chair and put his legs up on the table.

He gulped a glass of milk, draining its contents, then belched with embellishment. Without grown-ups around, his manners grew even worse.

"*My* father is the richest man in New York," Shirley bragged.

"No, he's not. Andrew Carnegie is the richest man in New York, everyone knows that," Cornelius corrected.

"Well, he's one of the richest. We have a mansion on Fifth Avenue that's even bigger than Frick's. He makes a lot of money on Wall Street." Shirley gracefully placed her napkin onto her lap. "How much does your Daddy make, Beatrice?"

"I have no idea. I'm only five-years-old. But we have a nice house in New Orleans," Bea downplayed the vast Manchester wealth. *It was just stuff, after all.*

"When I grow up, I'm going to marry the son of one of the wealthiest families in America. Or, I'm going to marry into nobility in England. Then I'll be a Lady, maybe even a Duchess or a Countess. Or I could be a princess in a European county," Shirley rambled about her future.

Giving into peer pressure, Bea couldn't stand it any longer, and said, "Well I saw a mermaid today."

Everyone laughed.

"Thank you for entertaining us with your overactive imagination," Shirley laughed.

Dinner finally arrived. A servant placed a plate with a small, whole cooked bird in front each of the children.

Cornelius tore off a leg and devoured it. Then he licked his fingers instead of using a napkin.

"What is this? How am I supposed to eat it, with my fingers?" Shirley asked with a revolted expression.

"It's a Cornish game hen—a delicacy in Scotland. It's quite tasty." Bea cut into the hen's breast and managed to eat without getting her hands dirty.

"Uh, Scotland is full of savages who are uncouth and uncivilized." Shirley refused to eat her Cornish game hen.

"That's not true. Have you ever even been to Scotland? It's beautiful. The Manchesters own a beautiful manor on the Isle of Skye. It's near Castle Garrison which is one of the most beautiful castles in Europe. I'm descended from the Earl of Garrison. In fact, I'm Lady Beatrice Manchester, but nobody calls me that, yet." Bea hated to brag to Shirley, but this spoiled brat needed to be put in her place. *Who does she think she is?* Bea prayed that Shirley found a husband in Europe so she'd never have to see her again.

With a snobbish tone, Shirley boasted, "Well, I'm not staying here the whole winter season. Next week, my parents are taking me to Europe. Then I'm sailing on the maiden voyage of the Titanic!"

Chapter Ten

Bea awoke to a giggling sound coming from her parents' adjoining room. The first rays of dawn flitted through the window of her pink bedroom. Her door creaked open, and Mommy and Daddy walked in.

"Oh, sorry, my dear, we didn't mean to wake you." Daddy sat on the bed.

"Bea, we just saw the most amazing sunrise. We walked to the beach and stood on the rocks while the sun rose across the ocean," Mommy said.

"Why are you up so early? And why are you still wearing the same dress from last night?" Bea asked.

"Oh, my dear. We never went to sleep. We stayed up all night with our friends and watched the sunrise. It was beautiful. But now we're going to bed."

"Can I go to the beach now to see the beautiful sunrise?" Hope filled Bea. She couldn't wait to search for her young merman.

"Of course, my dear. Good night, I mean, good morning." Daddy kissed her forehead and futilely tucked her in for the night.

Bea pulled off her covers and dressed in record time. Ignoring her hunger pains, she raced out the door. Running downstairs, she stopped at a large table filled with food.

Guests, still wearing their finery from the night before, ate from the buffet spread for breakfast.

Bea grabbed a small loaf of bread, an apple, and a chunk of cheese. Placing these in her knapsack, she scurried out the front door and ran towards the sea.

Just as her parents described, the sun rose on the horizon. It's rays quickly brightened the morning sky. Sun beams flitted on the water's surface, illuminating the ocean. Water swirled around the rocks as the tide went out, then it rushed back in, splashing Bea with a salty spray.

She sat on the rocks and retrieved the bread from her knapsack. Tearing the bread in chunks, she added a piece of cheese and gobbled it down. She bit into her green apple and relished its sour taste.

Scanning the surface, she hoped to find her merman. Finishing the last of her apple, she tossed the core into the sea. It descended into the clear water. Tiny fish swarm around the core, pecking it.

Singing echoed from the water. Perplexed, Bea dunked her face into the water. The most beautiful voices sang. Recognizing the Latin lyrics, she wondered what sort of sea creatures sang the dead language.

Colorful fish swam underwater, singing happily. These mesmerizing creatures were about the size of her thumb. They resembled the fairies she'd learned about from the *Book of Magical Creatures*. Only these sea fairies had thick wings which moved more like fish fins in the water.

Unable to hold her breath any longer, Bea lifted her face out of the water, took several deep breaths, then slid her face back into the chilly water.

Three underwater fairies studied her face. Their wings glowed beautiful neon colors—pink, green, and yellow. The fairies pointed to her, and the pink one asked, "Can you see us?"

Bea nodded, unable to speak underwater with any clarity.

"Are you magical, too?" the yellow one asked.

Nodding again, Bea blinked, unable to comprehend the beautiful sea sprites swimming before her. Then she recalled the large section from the *Book of Magical Creatures—Fairies and Sea Sprites*.

Chapter Eleven

"We didn't believe him," the pink sea sprite said. She swam around the others and studied Bea.

"Her eyes! Look, Ella and Della." The yellow one pointed to Bea.

"You're right, Ida," Della, the green sprite, said.

Bea lifted her face out of the water, just long enough to fill her lungs. Plunging her face back into the water, she kept her mouth just above the surface. She needed to breathe, but more importantly, she needed to talk to these beautiful sea sprites.

"Ella, Della, and Ida. It's nice to meet you. My name is Beatrice Manchester, but everyone calls me, Bea."

Ella, the pink one, swam directly in front of Bea, mesmerized by Bea's magical eyes. "Of course, you're magical. You're a Manchester with one green eye and one blue eye."

"But how did Peter know this human was magical?" Della asked.

"Good question. He couldn't possibly have been close enough to see her magical eyes, let alone know that she was a Manchester." Ida pondered.

"Who is Peter?" Bea asked, still awed in the presence of three beautiful sea sprites.

"You don't know who Peter is? The way he went on and on about you last night, we thought he'd known you forever." Della asked with a perplexed expression.

Shrugging, Bea said, "I've never met anyone named Peter, at least I don't think so."

"Last night at the palace, Peter came back from a long swim. His father was miffed that he was late for supper, again. Triton yelled, then warned him not to go near the shore. Peter swore that he didn't, but later that evening, he told us the truth," Ella explained.

"Excuse me, did you just say, Triton? And palace?" Bea knew the name, everyone did. But shock filled her. If Peter's father was Triton, then...she was right about what she saw yesterday. Now she knew who Peter was.

"Yes, of course. King Triton lives in the palace. He's Prince Peter's father," Ida said, matter-of-factly.

"Ah, now I know who Peter is. I saw him swimming here yesterday. But we never actually met. He just splashed me, then swam away with periodic flips in the air." Bea recalled the young merman with blond hair who'd captivated her heart.

"You haven't met Peter yet? He went on and on about the beautiful witch girl with long, black hair. He said you were the most beautiful creature he'd ever seen. We were a little insulted. I mean, look at us. We're gorgeous sea sprites." Ella waved her arms at Della and Ida.

"Yes, you three *are* beautiful creatures. But why couldn't Peter talk to me yesterday? Why did he swim away if I captivated him?" Bea asked.

"Ah, it's forbidden," Ida said.

"What's forbidden?" Bea asked.

"It is forbidden for Peter's kind to interact with humans. It's too dangerous. Mermaids have been murdered by humans for centuries," Della explained.

"But what about the one exception? Remember Triton's ancestor?" Ella asked.

"That's right. They could be the exception. But that would mean.....No impossible. Or is it?" Ida's expression grew hopeful.

Ella, Della, and Ida stared at Bea with amazed expressions. Smiling, they swam around gleefully singing.

"What? What's the exception?" Bea asked, consumed by the sea sprites' elation.

"You'll see. We don't want to spoil it for you. It should happen naturally." Ella beamed.

"It's okay, Peter. You can show yourself." Ida smiled.

Chapter Twelve

"Well, it's about time!" Peter hollered.

Something fast moved in the water, straight towards Bea and the sea sprites.

Bea removed her face from the water and studied the swirling disturbance.

The surface broke, and the young merman jumped into the air performing a perfect back flip. When this magnificent creature hit the surface, his large teal fin splashed water all over Bea.

"Goodbye, Bea." Ella, Della, and Ida waved, then swam away.

Bea waved back. "Goodbye. I hope to see you again." Bea sat on the rock and waited for her merman to appear.

A blond head broke the surface. Long locks clung to his shoulders. Bright teal eyes studied her through a handsome cherub-like face.

"Hello, you must be Peter." Bea smiled.

Nodding, he said, "Hello."

"My name is Beatrice Manchester, but everyone calls me, Bea."

"Like the insect? Which pollinates flowers?" Peter asked.

Laughing, Bea nodded. "Yes, it's pronounced like the insect, but spelled differently."

"How old are you? I'm eight." Peter asked. Leaning back, he floated on the surface, revealing his beautiful fin with shimmering, teal scales.

"I'm five. You have the most beautiful eyes. They match your fin." Bea smiled.

He lightly tapped his fin on the surface, sending ripples towards her.

"You have beautiful eyes, too. They're magical." His intense stare bored into hers.

"Yes, I'm a good witch from a very powerful coven. These eyes mean I will have great powers one day." Bea rubbed her arms, now prickled with goosebumps from the cold breeze blowing on her recently splashed on skin.

"Do you have any powers now?" Peter asked, obviously curious about her kind.

"I can start a fire," she boasted. "Here, watch." Rubbing her hands together, she cupped them like a ball. A fireball appeared, hovering just above her palm. Its orange flames warded off the chill.

"Cool." Giggling, he splashed it, instantly extinguishing Bea's ball of flame.

"Hey, that's not very nice." Pouting, she made another fireball.

"Sorry, I don't see fire too often. Only when I go to the surface, which I'm not supposed to do," he confessed.

"That's okay. Daddy says if a boy teases you, it means he likes you." Bea blushed.

Smiling, he nodded. "Where do you live?"

"In New Orleans. It's far away from here. My family and I are just visiting for the winter," Bea explained.

"Winter?"

"Winter is up north where it gets very cold and snows. That's why people want to come to Florida in the winter, to get out of the cold."

"That must be why the water up north is much colder than down here."

"Where do you live?" she asked.

"In a palace. It's under the sea on the ocean floor. It's far from here. I swam many leagues to get here. But I can swim really fast," Peter bragged.

"Are there a lot of mermaids in the ocean?" Bea gestured towards Peter's magnificent fin.

"Thousands, but not as many as there used to be. Humans sometimes catch us in their fishing nets. That's why I'm not supposed to go to the surface."

"I'm glad you did. I wish I could see your palace and the other mermaids." Bea sighed.

"If only you could breathe underwater." Peter sighed, too.

Recalling the tale from the *Book of Legends*, Bea beamed, "I know a way. All I need is a Chromium Cauldron."

Chapter Thirteen

"I've heard of the Chromium Cauldron." Peter's face beamed with delight.

"But do you know the legend?" Bea asked. She prayed the chapter Grandpa Bart read to her from the *Book of Cauldrons* was true. Now she wondered if just hearing about the legend a few days ago was a coincidence. But in her magical world, she knew that things were never a coincidence. Coincidences were usually fate.

Shrugging, he said, "I've only *heard* of the cauldron. Rumors flew that my ancestor had one."

"Do you think you could find it? Perhaps ask the sea sprites—Ella, Della, and Ida?" The notion of using the Chromium Cauldron to breathe underwater thrilled her. She'd love to swim in the ocean and see the mermaids and this beautiful palace Peter raved about.

"Okay, I will ask them tonight. Tell me more about this, cauldron." Peter's expression grew fascinated.

"Well, according to the *Book of Cauldrons*, a mermaid may present a Chromium Cauldron to a human to enable them breathe underwater," Bea recited the legend.

"Huh, I'm surprised that doesn't happen more often. Perhaps since humans terrify us, we're afraid to give them a cauldron." Peter glanced up, contemplating the notion.

"It can't just be any human that can use the cauldron. It must be presented to a witch or a wizard. A special potion must be brewed and a spell must be cast yielding the power of the Chromium Cauldron."

"You're a witch! You can cast the spell. Do you remember the potion's ingredients?" Peter's tone grew excited. "I'd love to take you underwater with me and show you the palace and the other mermaids."

"I can't remember the potion. The spell book I need is at home in New Orleans." Bea sighed.

"Is it far? Can you go and get the book?" Peter asked.

"New Orleans is far away. But there is a magical travel spell that witches and wizards can use to travel instantaneously. It's called, *Eo Ire Itum*. It's from the Latin word, 'to travel.'" Bea contemplated the spell. She'd never cast one herself, but she watched her parents cast spells all the time.

"Cool. Can you get the book and potion ingredients to cast the Chromium Cauldron spell?" Peter's teal eyes glistened. He was obviously smitten with her.

"I don't know? I've never traveled alone before." Bea worried. She wasn't supposed to use magic alone. Her parents warned her repeatedly of the danger. Although Grandma Olivia told her that when Violet was six, she used the Cobalt Cauldron to summon the spirit of her reincarnated soul mate—Tutankhamun.

"Can you try it, now?" Peter asked.

"I'm not supposed to use magic alone. It's dangerous," Bea recited her parents' strictest rule.

"And I'm not supposed to go to the surface, or the shore, or talk to humans. Yet here I am." Peter pressured her.

"I still haven't told you about the last condition of the Chromium Cauldron spell." Dropping her head, Bea blushed.

"What is it?" Peter studied her with a curious, yet hopeful expression. Like he somehow knew the last condition and already accepted his destiny, their destiny.

"A mermaid can only present the Chromium Cauldron to his or her one true love."

Chapter Fourteen

"Mommy, Daddy, wake up!" Bea ran into her parents' room through the adjoining door.

"What time is it?" Violet asked.

"Time to wake up." Bea shoved her father's shoulder, trying to wake him up.

"Huh, Bea? Why are you waking us up so early? We didn't go bed until dawn." Daddy turned and placed the pillow over his head to block the morning sun shining through the window.

"Oh, sorry. I forgot." Bea shrugged. She didn't care if she woke up her parents. It served them right for staying up all night. They made her go to bed early, even though she wanted to stay up with the grown-ups. Besides, she woke them up to help her practice magic. She could've just used magic alone, but she heeded their serious warning.

"What's so important that couldn't wait until we woke up?" Violet asked, still lying in bed.

"I saw three sea sprites and a young merman!" Bea squealed.

"Uh, huh." Mommy and Daddy mumbled. "Mermaids and sea sprites."

"Really. I'm not making this up. I saw the young merman yesterday when I went to the beach to collect sea shells. I told Grandpa Bart. He believed me."

"Uh, huh." Mommy turned her face into the pillow.

"Then just now, I went to the beach. I saw three sea sprites in the water. They were so beautiful. They looked like fairies, but their wings were fins. Their names were Ella, Della, and Ida."

"Uh, huh. Fins instead of wings," Daddy mumbled.

"I met Peter, who is actually Prince Peter. He's eight-years-old with blond hair and teal eyes. His fin is beautiful with shimmering teal scales which match

40

his eyes." Bea's tone grew excited just talking about her young merman, who may be her one true love.

"Uh, huh, Prince Peter, teal eyes," Mommy mumbled.

"Peter's father is Triton, King of the Mermaids."

"Uh, huh, Mermaid King," Daddy mumbled.

"They live in a beautiful palace on the ocean floor."

"Palace, ocean, uh, huh."

"There is a spell that uses a Chromium Cauldron which allows a witch to breathe underwater."

"Breathe, cauldron, uh, huh."

"You don't believe me, do you?" Bea asked, miffed that her parents doubted her. She'd never told a fib in her life. *Why wouldn't they believe her?*

Mommy winked to Daddy. "Of course, we believe you."

Daddy winked back.

"I need the *Book of Cauldrons* from the attic at home. I need the ingredients to make the potion to cast the spell with the Chromium Cauldron."

"Do you have the cauldron?" Daddy asked.

"No, but Peter is going to find one. The mermaids keep them hidden in the ocean," Bea explained. "Can you please take me home to the attic?" Holding her tiny hands in prayer, she pleaded.

"Maybe later, we want to sleep." Daddy yawned.

"Can Grandpa Bart take me? He's the one who read me the legend of the Chromium Cauldron."

"Sure. As long as you're not practicing magic alone, then it is fine with us." Violet yawned.

"Can he help me cast the spell with the Chromium Cauldron so I can breathe underwater?"

"Uh, huh." Mommy and Daddy drifted back to sleep.

Chapter Fifteen

"Yippee!" Bea ran out of her parents' room, down the hallway, and knocked on her grandparents' door.

"Good morning, my early bird." Grandpa Bart stood, already dressed for the day.

"Grandpa, can you take me back home? I need the *Book of Cauldrons*. Mommy and Daddy said it was okay if you go with me," Bea pleaded.

"Sure, but what do you need the book for?" Bart knelt and studied Bea.

"I need the potion and spell for the Chromium Cauldron. Remember the young merman I saw yesterday? I met him today. He's trying to find the cauldron. He wants to show me his palace. I need the cauldron to breathe underwater." Bea bounced excitedly.

"Ah, the legend is true. They usually are. And your parents said this was okay?" Bart asked.

"Yes, but they were half asleep. I don't think they believed me. Please, Grandpa," she begged.

"Fine, but we better hurry before your grandmother wakes up and nixes the mission."

"Yippee!" Bea grabbed Grandpa's hand. "Can I try?"

"Of course, my dear."

"*Eo Ire Itum*, Manchester Mansion attic, New Orleans," Bea chanted excitedly.

They instantly appeared in the attic of their home in New Orleans.

"You did it, my dear." Bart beamed, obviously proud of her growing powers.

"Yippee! I have more powers. Now, where is that book?" Bea rested her index finger on her chin while she scanned the book spines on the shelf next to the fireplace. "Ah, here it is, the *Book of Cauldrons*."

"Here, allow me. It's rather heavy." Grandpa pulled the large book off the shelf and carried it to the podium.

Bea climbed onto the wooden soap box and turned the pages with reverence.

"Here it is." She quietly studied the Latin words beautifully scribed in the book.

"Do we have all the ingredients?" Grandpa asked.

Walking to the potions shelf, Bea studied the glass vials. "Yes, we do. But we're low on dragon shrooms. Why are dragon shrooms so hard to get again?"

"Dragon shrooms must be harvested after a fire breathing dragon burns growing mushrooms. We better not use the rest of it or your grandmother will kill me," Grandpa grimaced.

"Oh, I can only cast the spell one time?" Bea asked. Disappointment filled her because she already knew the answer.

"I'm afraid so, my dear. You better make the most of your visit with the mermaids. I'm envious. I would love to see the mermaids."

Bea carefully copied the spell and potion instructions onto a piece of parchment. "I know we're not supposed to remove the book from the attic."

"Good girl. We wouldn't want a nonmagical human to discover it. Nor can we risk losing the book," Grandpa explained.

"Plus, it's too heavy to carry." Bea grabbed the six vials she needed and gently placed them in her knapsack, along with the parchment containing the spell of the Chromium Cauldron.

"Got everything?" Grandpa grabbed her hand and asked.

Nodding, she asked, "Ready?"

Grandpa nodded.

"*Eo Ire Itum*, Whitehall pink room, Palm Beach, Florida," Bea chanted.

Chapter Sixteen

At sunset, Bea stood on the rocks by the shore, waiting impatiently for Peter to appear.

"How long can I stay with Peter?" Bea asked Grandpa Bart, who held her hand and waited on the rocks with her.

"How long does the spell last?" He studied the ocean water.

"Twenty-four hours." Bea recalled.

"Good thing you took a long nap this afternoon since you'll be gone for twenty-four hours." He winked.

"Oh, thank you, Grandpa." Bea hugged him.

"If he ever gets here with the cauldron." His tone rang with impatience.

Peter emerged from the water, flipped in the air, and splashed Bea and Grandpa.

"Peter!" Bea squealed with delight.

A blond head broke the water's surface. Two hands appeared holding the Chromium Cauldron. Its silver color shone, and the setting sun's rays glistened off the ornate carvings.

"It's beautiful." Bea beamed.

"Ahem." Grandpa cleared his throat.

"Oh, sorry. Peter, this is my grandfather, Bart Manchester. Grandpa, this is His Royal Highness, Prince Peter."

Grandpa bowed, and Peter nodded.

Peter placed the cauldron on the rocks.

Bea studied the cauldron. It was bigger than the ones her parents had. Its rim was nearly three feet wide. Two ornate handles curved up over the rim. Picking it up, Bea said, "It's heavy, much bigger than I thought."

"Did you get the spell and potion?" Peter asked.

"Yes, but I only have enough ingredients to use the spell once. For the next twenty-four hours, I'll be able to breathe underwater," she explained.

"Fantastic, that's plenty of time to get to my palace and back." Peter raised his fin, then splashed the water's surface.

Bea opened the folded parchment and reread the ingredients. She poured sea water into the cauldron, then added the potion ingredients. Lifting the heavy cauldron in the air, she chanted the spell. Then she drank the contents of the cauldron.

"How do we know if it worked?" Grandpa asked.

Bea shrugged and said, "I'll just open my mouth underwater and see if I can breathe." She stepped into the water, and it chilled her. "Brrr, it's cold."

"You'll get used to it." Peter splashed her.

Bea walked into the water. Small waves splashed her. Once she was waist deep in the ocean, she ducked underwater and opened her eyes.

Peter's beautiful form appeared before her. His long blond hair floated around his cherub face. His teal fin swayed back and forth.

"Go ahead, try to breathe." Bubbles escaped Peter's mouth.

Opening her mouth, Bea let the water in. She gagged as water filled her mouth and lungs. Coughing, she fought the urge to rise out of the water. Once the water filled her, she no longer struggled for air. Somehow, the Chromium Cauldron spell converted the sea water into oxygen which allowed her to breathe.

"It's working, I'm breathing underwater!" Bea squealed.

Grandpa appeared above her. She gave him a thumbs up, nodded, and smiled.

Grandpa smiled back, waved, and said, "Have fun, my dear."

Chapter Seventeen

"This is so cool!" Bea breathed underwater.

"Come on, it's a long way to swim to the palace. It's dozens of leagues away." Peter grabbed her hand.

"What's the best way to do this?" Bea studied Peter's fin.

"You can ride on my back. Just wrap your arms around my chest." Peter held out his arms.

Bea swam behind him and wrapped her arms around his chest. Hugging him, she let his warmth soak into her chilled skin.

Peter flipped his teal fin and swam them towards the open waters of the Atlantic Ocean. He hovered near the bottom of the ocean floor which deepened the further they got out to sea. A huge drop off appeared, but Peter didn't go over it. Instead, he turned right and swam south, parallel to the shore.

Sea creatures studied them with curiosity. Colorful fish darted out of the way as they swam over coral waving in their wake.

"It's the coral reef." Peter pointed. "Be careful not to touch it. It's sharp and will slice your skin."

"It's beautiful." Colorful coral lined the ocean floor resembling tiny sea mountains.

"We're in the Keys, tiny islands off the coast of southern Florida. Some mermaids often swam here. But then humans arrived and built a train to the end of the Keys." Peter grumbled. "We're scared of humans."

Bea didn't share that she arrived in Palm Beach via that same train. Even worse, she stayed in the home of the man who'd built it.

"Where is the palace?" Bea asked.

"It's just off the coast of Cuba which is only ninety miles south of the southernmost Key. The beautiful, thriving city was once above water. Then the Gods were angered by the humans flourishing on the island. So the Gods sank it. Only the top of the mountains in Cuba are above the water, the rest is below. After the island sank, the mermaids moved into the palace," Peter explained.

They swam past the coral reef of the Florida Keys, and continued south. They hovered near the ocean floor, passing many boats resting on the sand. Bea felt safer knowing what was below them.

Pointing to the sunken ships, Peter said, "Poseidon's handiwork. When the God of the sea loses his temper, he sinks ships. Sometimes humans on boats will catch a mermaid and try to show other humans that we really exist. When that happens, Poseidon sinks their ship, kills all the humans aboard, and frees the mermaid.

A huge whale swam above them, hopefully unaware of their presence. The water grew darker as the sun set above the surface. Then light shone ahead.

"We're getting close." Peter nodded.

Bright gold illuminated the water. Tall columns supported the golden mountain. Pillars made of gold rose from the ocean floor, at least one hundred feet tall. Mermaids swam about, darting around the columns of the palace. Tiny entranceways were scattered throughout the golden mountain.

Awed, Bea said, "It's beautiful."

Peter swam them through an entrance in the gold mountain. Once through, an enormous courtyard opened up. A sunken city filled the courtyard, protected on all sides by a circular mountain of gold.

Recalling the stories Grandpa read from the *Book of Legends*, Bea asked. "Is this...?"

Beaming, Peter nodded, "Welcome to Atlantis!"

Chapter Eighteen

"Atlantis! I can't believe I'm here." Bea swam in awe next to Peter.

Hundreds of mermaids swam about Atlantis, darting around the gold pillars playfully.

"This is my home." Peter waved his arm up towards the highest point of the golden mountain beneath the sea.

"Can you show me?" Bea asked.

"Of course, the palace is near the top of Atlantis." Peter gestured for her to wrap her arms around his chest again.

Obliging, she held on tight while Peter swam them up to the highest point in Atlantis. They entered a large hall. Dozens of mermaids lounged and ate kelp. At the end of the hall sat a large merman upon a golden throne.

Peter released Bea, and they swam towards the throne. Other mermaids bowed when they swam by.

Arriving at the base of the throne, Peter bowed to Triton, King of the Mermaids. "Your Majesty."

Bea bowed, too.

"Rise, my son." Triton waved his golden scepter. A gold crown rested on his head of long, white hair. His long, white beard partially covered his massive, muscled chest. His long teal fin flapped against the base of the throne.

"Father, may I introduce Beatrice Manchester," Peter said.

Bea curtsied. "Your Majesty."

"Ah, you must be related to Mordecai Manchester. I recognize those magical eyes," Triton said.

"I've heard legends of him, he was a great-great-great uncle." Bea recalled the tale.

"He married my great-grandmother on my mother's side. In fact, she presented him with the same Chromium Cauldron. I'm glad it still works," Triton chuckled.

"Where did they live?" Bea asked, curious about the logistics of an interspecies marriage.

"Mordecai invented a spell to turn her fin into legs whenever they wanted to go above the surface," Triton explained.

"They lived both here *and* on land?" Bea asked.

"Yes, but they didn't live in Scotland with the other Manchesters. They started a colony on the island of Martinique. They built a beautiful plantation and harvested sugar cane. Scotland was too far away from Atlantis. Besides, the water is freezing up there." Triton shivered.

"I've heard of the Martinique Manchesters, but I've never visited there. Did they have babies?" Bea asked.

"No, they did not. But we all wondered if any offspring would have a fin. I think they realized that they couldn't have babies because mer*maids* lay eggs. But in the case of a mer*man* and a human female...." Triton paused, then winked. "Well, I'll explain when you're older, son."

Bea turned to Peter and asked, "Will you be King one day?"

Peter shook his head. "No, I have dozens of older brothers and sisters."

"And I plan on living a long time." Triton grinned.

"Your Majesty," Ella, Della, and Ida said in unison and bowed before the king.

"Rise my beautiful sea sprites. What brings you to Atlantis?" Triton asked.

With a worried expression, Ida spoke, "It's the Gods. They're angry with the humans."

"They're always angry with the humans. That's why they sank Atlantis," Triton said.

"Well, we heard from Poseidon that the Gods are jealous of the wealthy humans. Zeus wants him to teach the humans a lesson again. Poseidon plans to sink the Titanic!"

Chapter Nineteen

"Huuuuuhhhh." Bea emerged from the water and breathed air for the first time in nearly twenty-four hours.

Peter emerged next to her, flipping his fin and splashing the water.

"Ah, air. I can breathe air again," Bea gasped, happy to be near land again, but sad that her twenty-four hours with Peter came to an end.

"I miss you already." Tears dropped on Peter's cheek.

"I know. I had the most amazing time. Atlantis is spectacular. The mermaids are amazing, beautiful creatures. They were very nice to me. I'm surprised, I thought they were scared of humans." Bea treaded water.

"We are. But since you could breathe underwater, and you were with me, Prince Peter, they weren't scared," he explained.

"I wish I had more dragon shrooms to make more potion for the Chromium Cauldron." She sighed.

"What? We can't use the spell again?" Peter asked. "And where is the Chromium Cauldron?" Peter scanned the shore.

"My grandpa probably has it. He'll keep it safe for me. Do you want it back?" Bea hated the notion of parting with the beautiful cauldron.

"No, you can keep it. When you get more dragon shrooms, we'll go back to Atlantis."

"Oh, thank you. When will I see you again?" she asked pleadingly.

"I don't know. I can try to come here again, but I'm not sure my father will let me. I'm probably going to be in big trouble for coming to the shore and meeting a human." He slumped.

"But what about your ancestor? She obviously went to the shore to meet my ancestor. Did she get in trouble then?" Bea asked.

"Oh, yeah, big time. But she was older, and the sea sprites convinced the Queen of the mermaids that they couldn't stop true love. So, it all worked out in the end." Peter's tone rang with optimism.

"Oh, do you think...? I mean....Do you think we're true loves?" Bea blushed.

"I hope so." Peter stared into her eyes and kissed her lips with a quick peck.

Euphoria consumed Bea. She was so happy she cried. "The legend says that the Chromium Cauldron will only work on true loves. And since it worked...."

"We are true loves. But our parents will never let us be together until we're older. What age to humans get married?" Peter asked.

"Sixteen, usually. I'm only five and a half. We have to wait over ten years to get married."

"But once we're married, our parents can't stop us from being together. Let's meet here again in ten years. In the meantime, find lots of dragon shrooms." Peter kissed her again.

Bea turned to the shore and the setting sun. What a beautiful sunset to seal the proposal of marriage with her one true love, Prince Peter, the young merman from Atlantis.

Bea studied the rocks on the shore. "Uh, oh."

"What's wrong?" Peter asked.

"It's my parents. They look worried, ...and really mad."

Chapter Twenty

"I'm out of here." Peter kissed Bea's cheek.

"No, don't leave me. You should meet my parents, especially if you want to marry me in ten years," Bea scolded.

Slumping defeatedly, he sighed, "Fine. I'll meet your parents."

Bea swam to the rocks, and Peter followed reluctantly. Her parents stood on the rocks and pointed at her in the water. Grandpa Bart stood behind them holding the Chromium Cauldron. Bea climbed out of the water.

Her parents ran to her and hugged her. "Oh, Beatrice Manchester. Thank the Gods you are unharmed. But you are in so much trouble, young lady," Mommy scolded.

"I'm just glad you are okay." Turning towards Peter, Daddy asked, "And who do we have here?"

"Mommy, Daddy, this is Prince Peter of Atlantis. Peter, these are my parents, Toliver and Violet Manchester," Bea said.

Peter, who floated next to the rocks, extended his hand and shook hands with her parents. "Mr. and Mrs. Manchester. It is a pleasure to meet you."

"Hello, do we...bow?" Mommy curtsied and bowed her head.

Daddy bent at the waist, dropped his head, and said, "Atlantis? You don't say. So, the legends are true." His eyebrow arched inquisitively.

Peter nodded.

Grandpa wrapped a towel over Bea's shoulders. "Here, you'll catch your death. Hello again, Prince Peter." Grandpa bowed.

"Here, come on out of the water, son." Daddy waved.

Peter shook his head, "Sorry, sir, but I can't."

Mommy and Daddy turned to one another with puzzled expressions. "Why not?"

Peter brought his enormous teal fin to the surface and gently splashed the water.

Mommy and Daddy's mouths gaped. "What the...? Are you...?" Mommy asked.

Peter nodded.

"Mommy, Daddy, Peter is a merman. He is also my true love." Bea smiled

Chapter Twenty-One

"Oh, my." Mommy clasped her hand over her heart.

"He's incredible." Daddy gasped.

Bea told her parents all about the Chromium Cauldron spell and her adventure to Atlantis with all the mermaids.

"That's incredible, but you're still in trouble for practicing magic without us," Mommy scolded.

"But you said I could if Grandpa Bart was with me." Bea stomped her foot and crossed her arms.

"We did?" Mommy shot Daddy a puzzled stare.

"Remember? I asked if I could go back home to study the *Book of Cauldrons* and gather the ingredients I needed to cast the spell. You were half asleep, but you nodded. Then I asked if Grandpa Bart could help me cast the Chromium Cauldron spell, and you nodded and said, 'Uh, huh.'"

"Did I?" Mommy asked Daddy.

"I think we did, my dear. But we'd been up all night and drank too much." Daddy lowered his head, obviously ashamed.

"Oh yeah." Mommy blushed, then turned to Grandpa. "And you.... How could you let her cast the spell and swim off into the ocean all night? What were you thinking?"

Grandpa's expression turned frightened. "She said, that *you* said it was okay. Besides, how could I deny our precious Beatrice the adventure of a lifetime— breathing underwater and seeing Atlantis and the mermaids."

"Argh, Dad, you have to stop spoiling my daughter. Would you have let me go?" she asked with a frustrated tone.

"Oh, hell no. But it's a grandparent's job to spoil their grandchildren." Bart chuckled.

"You know, I always told myself I wouldn't be as overprotective as you were with me, but now I am. I can't believe I'm going to do this, but you did the same thing to me when I was Bea's age. You took the Cobalt Cauldron away from me when I was six. I was so angry because I couldn't summon Toliver's, a.k.a. King Tut's, spirit." Violet turned to Toliver and touched his cheek.

Daddy nodded with reluctance.

Bea's mind scrambled to decipher what Mommy meant. Then she recalled her parents' tale about the Cobalt Cauldron. "No!"

Mommy took the Chromium Cauldron from Grandpa Bart's hands. "I'm sorry, my dear. But we're going to take this until you are older," Mommy said.

"But how will I see Peter?" Bea cried.

"He can come visit in New Orleans. Don't forget we live by the sea, too," Mommy rationalized.

"Now say your goodbyes while we slowly walk back to Whitehall." Daddy turned.

Bea jumped back into the water with Peter. "Oh, my love. Will you come see me in New Orleans?"

"Yes, of course, my love. Then in ten years, on your sixteenth birthday, we can marry." Peter kissed Bea on the lips.

With tears dropping on her cheeks, she said, "In the meantime, I'm going to scour the earth and gather as much dragon shrooms as possible. Then, when we marry, I'll be able to breathe underwater for the rest of my life."

"Goodbye, my love." Peter kissed her again, swam away, and flipped into the air one last time with an enormous splash.

Chapter Twenty-Two

The entourage entered Whitehall at dusk. Violet stepped into the vast foyer carrying the Chromium Cauldron wrapped in a towel. Toliver held his hand protectively on his wife's lower back, and Bea and Grandpa Bart stood behind them.

"Where is everybody? Why is it so eerie in here?" Bea asked.

"The sun just set, and the servants haven't turned on the lamps yet. Everyone is upstairs resting before dinner," Daddy said.

Mary Flagler gracefully descended the left marble staircase. Already dressed for dinner, she wore a red gown with a small train. A beautiful ruby necklace adorned her neck.

"Oh, you're downstairs early. Forgive me for not being here to greet you. I came down early to check on dinner and ensure they set the table according to my impeccable standards. I'm very particular. I want my birthday celebration to be perfect." Mary smiled.

"Happy Birthday, Mrs. Flagler." Bea curtsied.

"Aren't you a dear and precious child." Mary turned to Bea's parents and said, "You must be very proud of your little girl."

"Thank you, and happy birthday, Mary." Violet slightly bowed her head.

Mary somehow mistook the nod of respect for the presentation of a gift. "Oh, you brought me a gift." She took the towel-wrapped cauldron from Violet's hands and removed the towel.

"But...." Bea tried to object.

"Oh, my, God! It's exquisite." Mary jumped excitedly. "It's the most beautiful thing I've ever seen."

"But..." Bea tried to object, but Mommy nudged her with a scowled expression.

Mary gushed, "Thank you very much. The silver bowl is beautiful with its ornate carvings. I need something to hold the wine during dinner since we drink so much of it. I have the perfect place for it. Follow me."

It's not a silver bowl, it's a Chromium Cauldron! Bea looked up at Mommy who must've read her mind because she held her index finger to her lips.

Anxiety raced through Bea and made her heart beat faster.

Was Mommy going to let Mary Flagler keep the Chromium Cauldron? The prospect was unfathomable. *How would she breathe underwater and visit Prince Peter?*

Mary led them through the music room and into the vast dining room. A long, exquisitely set table dominated the room. The long, green rug beneath the table coordinated perfectly with the green velvet covering the cushioned dining room chairs. Dark, mahogany wood paneling covered the lower half of the walls while beautiful, green damask wallpaper covered the upper half. Beautiful, intricately designed wood inlays decorated the coffered ceiling.

Mary walked to the left of the table and placed the cauldron on a mahogany side table. "Perfect. I'll let the staff know to pour the wine in it before dinner."

Nooooooo! Bea screamed inside her head. Tears dropped uncontrollably on her cheeks. *It was her cauldron. Peter gave it to her. How dare her parents let Mary keep it.*

She ran upstairs to her pink bedroom, plopped on the bed face down into her pillow, and cried uncontrollably. "Noooooo! My Prince, my true love. How can we get married if I can't breathe underwater?"

Chapter Twenty-Three

Bea shot up in bed to find her parents sitting on the bed with her.

"Oh, sorry to wake you, my dear. We wanted to check on you. Are you hungry? You missed dinner." Daddy asked.

"My tummy aches. I'm too upset to eat. How could you let her keep the Chromium Cauldron? It's not yours to give away. Prince Peter gave it to *me*. It's mine," she whined with a pathetic tone, drained from exhaustion.

"There, there. It's for the best. Besides, you don't have any dragon shrooms to cast the spell," Mommy said.

"But I can find some. Surely the Manchesters in Scotland can harvest them. They have a fire breathing dragon after all."

"But you're too young to go to Atlantis with Peter. Wait until you're older. If he is your true love, then destiny will bring you two together again. Trust me. It brought your father and me together again, and again, again." Mommy beamed at Daddy.

"Over the next ten years, we'll collect enough dragon shrooms that you can live with Peter in Atlantis for the rest of your life," Daddy promised.

The thought of marrying Peter in ten years and living in Atlantis with the mermaids cheered her up. She wiped her eyes and nodded.

"There, there. That's my big girl. I know you're excited about spending the rest of your life with Peter, and you can't wait to grow up. But trust me. Being an adult is hard work. We have responsibilities and worries. I miss the carefree days of my youth when my biggest decision was which doll to play with." Mommy hugged her.

"Your mother is right. In fact, my first childhood was even shorter. I ascended the throne of Egypt at the age of nine. I had to grow up real fast and rule a country. I constantly feared conspiracies to assassinate me," Daddy said.

"Don't you like your life now?" Bea asked.

Smiling, Mommy grabbed her hand. "Well of course, I love my nine lives with you and your father. But your childhood is precious. Remember to enjoy every last minute of it because you're already growing up too fast."

Bea nodded, then wiped the last of her tears with her sleeve.

"Do you want something to eat?" Mommy asked.

Shrugging, she said, "I'm not hungry. My tummy still aches, and I feel like I'm supposed to help with something." Bea rubbed her belly.

"I'm sure it will come to you. That feeling gets worse when you get older," Daddy chuckled.

Bea grasped her throat. "Mommy, Daddy, I remember. We have to warn everyone about the Titanic. The Gods are angry and want to sink the ship."

Chapter Twenty-Four

Days later

"Good morning, sweetheart." Daddy held a breakfast tray, and Mommy held something behind her back.

Sunlight poured through the window of the pink bedroom. Bea used to jump out of bed, eager to start the day. But ever since Mary Flagler took the Chromium Cauldron, Bea lounged in bed, deeply depressed. She missed Peter terribly. Her heart ached for him, longing to be with her true love.

Daddy removed last night's untouched dinner tray from the nightstand and replaced it with the breakfast tray. Lifting the silver dome lid, he said, "Voila."

Bea studied the plate of sunny-side-up eggs, bacon, and bread. But the thought of food repulsed her. Her stomach ached almost as much as her heart.

"Beatrice, please eat something. It's been three days since you last ate. You could die if you don't eat something soon," Mommy warned.

"I don't feel like eating. I just want to see my prince." A tear dropped on her cheek.

Daddy changed the subject. "We tried to warn the other guests about the Titanic, but no one would listen. Everyone swears that the ship is unsinkable. Several guests are leaving this week to travel to England just to sail back on Titanic's maiden voyage."

Bea thought of that annoying girl, Shirley Morgan, glad that she was sailing on the Titanic. "I guess we can't reveal how we know that Poseidon plans to sink the ship without revealing our magic."

"Oh, I almost forgot. We have something for you." Mommy removed her arms from behind her back. A tiny ball of orange, black, and white fur curled up in Mommy's hands.

"A kitten." Bea took the tiny kitten and looked into eyes which matched her own—one blue and one green. She wasn't as excited as she'd thought she'd be. She'd wanted a kitten for as long as she could remember, but now that she held one, her spirits were still deeply depressed.

"It's a calico. Mary's cat had kittens two months ago. Now that they're weaned from their mother, she is giving them away," Daddy explained.

"Hello, kitty." Bea held the beautiful creature in her hands.

"What will you name her?" Mommy asked.

Bea shrugged, laid back down, and closed her eyes.

Mommy and Daddy each kissed her forehead.

Exhaustion filled Bea, and she drifted off to sleep.

Her parents whispered to one another. "What are we going to do? Bea hasn't eaten in three days. She was thin before, but look at her now, she's just skin, bones, and hair." Mommy's tone sounded sad, like she was crying.

"I know. I'm terrified, too. We could lose our baby girl." Daddy's voice sounded sad, too.

"What about the Copper Cauldron?" Daddy asked, referring to the spell which enabled a witch or wizard to utilize their nine lives.

"It would work, but with her deep depression, she'd use all nine lives like that." Mommy snapped her fingers.

"I thought for sure the kitten would cheer her up. She desperately wanted one. I even promised her one when we returned to New Orleans," Grandpa Bart said.

I didn't know Grandpa Bart was here? Bea kept her eyes closed.

64

"Dad, please help us. We can't lose our Baby Bea," Mommy cried.

"Your mother, Olivia, *Eo Ire Itumed* back home to consult the *Book of Spells*. She has an idea to save our Baby Bea," Grandpa explained.

"What's her idea? We're desperate. I'll do anything to save her," Daddy pleaded.

Grandma Olivia instantly appeared, kicking her legs to ward off the cramps which accompanied *Eo Ire Itum*.

"Speak of the devil," Grandpa said.

"Mom, did you find anything?" Violet asked.

"Yes, it's extreme. But I think it will save our Baby Bea," Grandma Olivia said.

"What is it? We'll do anything to save her." Mommy asked.

"The problem is her heart is breaking, and she's lost the will to live. That's why she's shutting down and not eating," Grandma explained.

"What about using the last of our dragon shrooms? Then she could see Prince Peter again." Daddy asked.

"That would only make things worse. The Chromium Cauldron spell would only work for one day. Then she'd love him even more. Once they parted again, she'd grow deeply depressed," Grandma said.

Peter. I want to see my prince again. Thoughts of Peter swam through Bea as she drifted in and out of consciousness.

"Are you sure you're willing to do anything?" Grandma asked Violet and Toliver.

"Yes, please. Otherwise she'll die," Mommy cried.

Grandma said, "I found a spell that will erase her memory."

Chapter Twenty-Five

10 years later
Mount Olympus

Zeus studied the mortals on Earth, shaking his head in frustration.

"They didn't learn, did they?" Poseidon stood next to Zeus on the edge of a cloud.

"Perhaps sinking the Titanic with an iceberg, brilliant idea by the way, wasn't enough."

"We didn't send a strong enough message, we just killed 1500 mortals. Some of them were poor servants and immigrants who didn't deserve to die. They just happened to be on board with the rich."

"Have you seen the east coast of Florida? They are destroying my once beautiful and pristine beaches by erecting gaudy mansions and hotels," Poseidon fumed. "And a railroad was built all along the east coast of Florida down to Key West."

"Can you create a giant tsunami?" Zeus asked.

"I have an idea." Poseidon led Zeus to the lagoon on Mount Olympus.

Poseidon twirled his trident in the water and blew on the whipping waves. The spiral storm destroyed a statue of humans on the other side of the lagoon.

"Brilliant, Poseidon." Zeus smiled.

"It's called a hurricane. I can create it, then force it to go wherever I wish."

"Make one, and destroy all those tacky homes the rich mortals built," Zeus ordered. "But this time, we must take credit for this imminent disaster. We want the mortals to know that they have angered the Gods by forgetting about us."

"I'll leak it to the mermaids," Poseidon said.

Chapter Twenty-Six

"Meow," Penelope, Bea's calico cat, cried.

Bea woke up in her bedroom at the Manchester Mansion in the Garden District of New Orleans. "Good morning, precious." Bea petted her beloved feline.

Penelope sat on Bea's chest, as she did every morning for the last ten years, and begged for her breakfast. "Meow."

"Arrgh, fine. Why do you insist on breakfast so early?" Bea begrudgingly crawled out of bed. After donning her violet silk robe, she trudged downstairs.

"Mornin'." Mom poured a cup of coffee in the kitchen.

"Good morning. This cat is hungry." Bea opened a can of tuna and plopped the pungent breakfast into Penelope's bowl. The beautiful calico cat purred as she ate the tuna.

"Try feeding her before bed so she won't be so hungry in the morning," Mom suggested, then poured Bea a cup of coffee and handed it to her.

"Thanks, I tried. But she still woke up at the crack of dawn with the sun. Where's Dad?" Bea sipped the hot coffee and relished the caffeine infusion.

"In the attic, puttering around as usual." Mom turned the page of the morning paper—*The New Orleans Advocate.*

"I'll go see what he's up to." Bea ascended the stairs, and Penelope followed her.

Arriving in the attic, Bea found her father sitting by the fire with the *Book of Demons* in his lap. "Good morning, Dad."

"Good morning, sweetheart. Cat woke you up early again?" Dad asked.

"With the sun. I can't wait until sunrise is later. Watcha studying?" Bea sat on the wing-back chair opposite her father and sipped her coffee. Penelope jumped onto her lap, circled around, then curled up for her post breakfast nap.

"I'm trying find this new demon I saw so I can figure out how to vanquish it. Tricky little booger." His right eyebrow arched with intrigue.

Bea studied the potion ingredients lining the shelves next to the fireplace. Dragon shrooms overflowed their glass jars. "Well, if vanquishing this new demon requires dragon shrooms, you're in luck. I see you got *even* more. Why so many?" Bea scratched Penelope's head.

"Well, since they're so hard to get, we asked our Manchester cousins in Scotland to harvest a bunch. When you were little, we almost ran out. Ever since then, we've stockpiled as much as possible. Luckily, they have a fire breathing dragon to make the dragon shrooms." Dad's tone turned apprehensive, like running out of dragon shrooms was a sore subject.

"I don't remember, but then again, I don't remember anything before I was six." Bea sighed.

Dad stood, placed the *Book of Demons* back on the shelf, and scratched Penelope's head. He was rewarded when she turned on her back and stretched, her subtle hint to rub her belly. "It's all her fault. When she was a kitten, she got stuck in that big oak tree out back. You climbed the tree to rescue her, slipped, and fell to the ground. Scared the dickens out of your mother and me. You woke up and couldn't remember a thing, not even who we were. The doctor said you had amnesia."

"Will I ever remember the first six years of life?" Bea asked.

Dad shrugged. "Amnesia is sometimes temporary, but the doctor said the longer your memory is gone, the less likely you are to regain it. It's looking more and more likely that you'll never remember. But most people don't remember much before the age of three anyway."

Something bothered Bea. Why does this story sound different this time? The tree. Then it hit her. "I thought Grandpa Bart said it was the oak tree in the *front* yard, the one with the branch that touches the house. He said that's how Penelope eventually got down. She jumped onto the roof, and he was able to fetch her through an open window."

Dad's expression grew worrisome, then contemplative. After a long pause, he said, "Grandpa Bart is old. His memory isn't what it used to be."

Bea grew suspicious, she was positive that's what Grandpa Bart had told her, and his mind was sharp as a tack. *Why was her father lying to her?*

Chapter Twenty-Seven

"Tea time." Mom hollered from the kitchen.

"I'm here." Bea had already arrived in the front parlor, along with the mid-afternoon sun. Sitting on the gold wing-back chair in front of the fire, she finally got her turn with the morning paper. The headline caught her attention.

Hurricane devastates Bermuda.

"Isn't it awful?" Dad peered over her shoulder.

Startled, she yelled, "Dad, don't sneak up on me like that." Bea clasped her hand over her heart.

"Sorry, my dear. You used to sneak up on us when you were little and scare the devil out of us." Dad walked over to the mahogany cabinet which served as a bar. He retrieved a Waterford Crystal tumbler and poured his afternoon Wild Turkey Kentucky Bourbon into the tumbler.

"Now *that* I remember because it was after I fell from the tree." Bea's attention turned to the article about the hurricane.

Mom walked in carrying a tray with tea and finger sandwiches. "Don't get up, Bea. We wouldn't want to disturb Her Royal Highness." She nodded to Penelope who napped on Bea's lap.

Bea stroked Penelope's fur with one hand and held the paper with the other. "It seems that there are more hurricanes this year."

"And stronger, too. They hit the islands hard and destroyed the crops. Many sugar cane farms were completely obliterated. Our Manchester cousins in Martinique threaten to come live with us." Mom poured a spoonful of sugar into her tea. Then she added honey and lemon into Bea's.

"You may have to switch to honey if there is a sugar shortage, my love." Dad raised his glass to his lips and drained the rest of his bourbon. Then he plopped a tiny sandwich into his mouth and hummed. "Mmmmm, pimento cheese, my favorite."

"Mine, too. Much better than those disgusting cucumber ones." Bea plopped the pimento goodness into her mouth.

"Okay, okay, you told me a thousand times and I haven't made cucumber sandwiches since. But just because it's green doesn't mean it tastes bad." Mom shot Bea a dirty look, referring to Bea's abhorrence of vegetables.

"At least we always know when a hurricane is coming, all of the critters move inland," Dad explained.

"And Penelope just loves catching all those snakes and bringing them inside as presents. Don't ya girl?" Bea rubbed Penelope's belly.

Without opening her eyes, Penelope rolled onto her back like a dead cockroach for a better belly rub.

"Well, since we're all here. There's something your mother and I wish to discuss with you." Dad set his glass down on the fireplace mantle.

Her parents stared at her strangely.

"What is it? Did someone die? Ya'll look so serious." Bea worried.

"We're going to North Carolina. Vanderbilt has bugged us for years to come see his Biltmore Estate in the Blue Ridge Mountains," Dad announced.

"Oh, is that all? Sounds like fun. What's so important about that?" Bea relaxed in her chair, relieved.

"You don't remember, but you met George Washington Vanderbilt when you were a little girl at Whitehall in Palm Beach, Florida. You also met his Vanderbilt relative, Cornelius. I get that family tree so confused." Dad shook his head.

"You're right, I don't remember. That was before my fall, right?" Bea asked.

"Yes, in fact, it was the same trip we gave you Penelope. She was one of the kittens Mary Flagler's cat had while we were there visiting Florida for the winter," Dad explained.

"Who else will be there?" Bea asked.

"Everyone. All the wealthy friends of the Vanderbilts and their children, many of whom are your age or slightly older." Mom gave her that strange look again.

"Why all the doom and gloom. What's going on?" Bea asked, angered and worried.

"We're going to the Biltmore to find you a husband," Mom proclaimed.

Chapter Twenty-Eight

The Manchesters arrived at the Biltmore in a motorcar which picked them up at the train station. The motorcar stopped at the top of the hill which provided a breathtaking view of the estate. Its stone exterior resembled the chateaus in France, only this was at least ten times bigger than any chateau Bea remembered. It's copper roof, now green, capped the estate with intricate roof lines. Gargoyles lined the rooftop, guarding the estate.

"Wow, for once, Vanderbilt wasn't embellishing." Dad stared, awestruck. "It's a shame old George passed away. His daughter, Cornelia, lives here now."

"It's amazing. How long are we staying for?" Bea asked.

"Long enough to find you a husband, my dear," Mom said.

"But I'm only fifteen. I'm too young to get married," Bea reasoned.

"Ah, but you will turn sixteen while we're here. They're planning a big party, too." Dad explained.

Bea froze. Her sixteenth birthday loomed ahead. But that's not what scared her. Something prickled the back of her brain, like a memory struggling to recover. She didn't know what, but something life changing was supposed to happen on her sixteenth birthday. And it wasn't supposed to happen at the Biltmore.

"But what about fate? What about true love? Something's nagging me about true love, but I can't put my finger on it." Bea asked.

Grandpa Bart turned white as a sheet. He looked to Toliver, like he needed his guidance.

Dad shook his head, then changed the subject. "Let's head down, shall we?"

"What? What is it? I know ya'll are hiding something." Bea stomped her foot.

"But Toliver, please. She has the right to know," Grandpa Bart begged.

"Dad, that's enough." Violet slipped her arm into her father's elbow.

"Tell me, Grandpa. Please?" Bea begged.

Bart gave Violet and Toliver a pleading expression.

Mom and Dad shook their heads vehemently.

"Bart, dear. You're getting tired and agitated. Remember your memory isn't what it used to be. You're confused. Let's go in and lie down," Grandma Olivia said soothingly.

"I'm not stupid! I know ya'll are keeping something important from me. And I'm going to find out!" Bea silently vowed to confront Grandpa when they were alone. He'd never deny her anything. *What were they hiding?*

Chapter Twenty-Nine

After settling into their rooms at the Biltmore, the Manchesters dressed in their finest and descended the massive stone staircase to mingle downstairs with the other guests.

The receiving room was an enormous long room, about the length of the hall of Mirrors in the Palace of Versailles in France. A huge marble fireplace focalized the room. Beautiful silk upholstered furniture was arranged in numerous sitting areas throughout the room. One wall was lined with windows and doors which led out onto a large stone terrace.

Bea stepped out onto the terrace and was greeted with a breathtaking view of the Blue Ridge Mountains. A cool breeze chilled her, a refreshing change from the hot, humid summer in New Orleans.

A tall, blonde-haired beauty flitted nearby. She looked familiar, but Bea couldn't place her. *Was she some socialite she'd seen in the paper?*

The blonde hung on the arm of a young man and laughed at his words. The man broke free, and walked inside. Now alone, the blonde, who wore a red gown showing too much bosom, spotted Bea and walked towards her.

"Hello, I love your frock. My name is Shirley Morgan." She extended her gloved hand to shake.

Bea looked down at her dated violet dress and winced. "Thank you. It's my mother's. She wore it the day she met my father. She thinks it's lucky and suggested I wear it to find a husband." Bea laughed.

"Well, stay away from the Vanderbilt heir, he's mine," Shirley scolded.

Déjà vu enveloped Bea. She remembered those words. *Had she met Shirley before? Were pieces of her lost memory returning at last?*

"I remember you. You're Beatrice Manchester, right?" the blonde asked.

"Well, yes. I'm sorry. You look familiar, but I can't place you. Have we met before?" Bea asked.

"We met at Whitehall ten years ago. I remember your beautiful eyes—one blue and one green," Shirley said.

"Oh, perhaps. Please forgive me, but I fell from a tree when I was five and lost my memory. But my parents told me that they took me to Whitehall shortly before that," Bea explained.

"Ah, I remember your parents, too. They told the scariest tale—the Titanic would sink. They begged my parents not to set foot on the doomed ship. Everyone thought they were crazy because the Titanic was unsinkable. But my mother, a superstitious sort, believed your parents and convinced my father to stay in Europe instead of sailing on the Titanic. I was so mad because I bragged to everyone that I was sailing on the maiden voyage of the most luxurious ship ever made. I was a bit of spoiled brat back then. But your parents saved our lives!" Tears dropped on Shirley's cheeks.

"Oh, I remember that awful tragedy when the Titanic sank, but I had no idea my parents somehow foresaw it. How fortunate that you and your family steered clear of the doomed vessel." Bea clasped Shirley's hand sympathetically. Something nagged at the back of her brain. *Another memory trying to come back?*

"If my memory serves me correctly, they said it was *you* who had a wild dream about it. How did you know?" Shirley asked.

Shrugging, she said, "Sorry, but I don't remember." But something else nagged at her. She knew about the Titanic, but it wasn't from a dream. *Somebody had told her, but who?*

"You told me the craziest story at dinner. You said that you met a young merman in the sea."

Chapter Thirty

Luckily, supper was served cocktail style. Bea couldn't fathom a dining room table big enough to seat over one hundred people.

Tuxedoed waiters carried bite-sized food on silver trays. Bea loved the shrimp cocktail the best. And the mushrooms stuffed with crab and cheese tasted divine, too. She held her third glass of champagne and decided to slowly sip this one because her head spun.

Five young gentlemen, dressed in their finest, surrounded her, all vying for her attention and place on her dance card. Euphoric, Bea counted her blessings to be surrounded by such wealthy heirs—an Astor, a Hershey a Rockefeller, a Carnegie, and a Vanderbilt. Her parents would approve, even though none of them were magical, like her.

"Beatrice, have you heard of the new dance called the Charleston? It's all the rage in New York." Jack asked. He was the son of a wealthy family who'd made a fortune on Wall Street.

"I have, but I've never tried it. I hear it's scandalous," Bea lied. Grandpa Bart told her all about the latest dance craze. She'd even practiced in her room each time the song came on this new contraption called the radio. But she didn't want her suitors to think she was fast and loose.

"Well, if they play it tonight, promise me you'll dance it with me," Jack pleaded. His big brown eyes were adorable.

"I promise." Bea smiled.

"You have the most beautiful eyes. I remember meeting you at Whitehall years ago. I'm afraid I was bit of a brat back then. Weren't you the one who dreamt about the Titanic sinking before it actually sank?" the young Vanderbilt gentleman asked.

"I don't remember, but I've been told that story. Apparently, it stopped other guests from boarding, thus saving their lives." Bea sipped her champagne and wished she could remember her life before the age of six.

"It stopped my father from boarding the Titanic," the Hershey heir said.

"Thank goodness, if Hershey stopped making their delicious chocolate, the world would come to an end," Bea said.

"Are you psychic? How did you know?" the young Astor asked.

"If you are psychic, what's the best stock to buy?" Jack asked.

"Who's going to win the world series this year? I'll place a bet if you know," the Astor heir asked.

Shrugging, she said, "I'm not psychic. If I was, I'd know which one of you handsome gentlemen to let court me." She winked.

Everyone laughed.

"Well, I'm sure it's not Peter. He's the poorest of the lot." The young Carnegie slapped his pal on the back.

Bea froze. *Peter? Why was that name familiar?* Her heart ached, like she'd lost somebody. *But who?*

"Miss Manchester? Are you all right? You turned white as a sheet?" Jack asked.

"You look like you've seen a ghost." Peter took her champagne flute away.

Startled back to reality, Bea said, "I, uh, excuse me, gentlemen. I'm afraid the champagne has gone to my head. I think I'll rest in the powder room."

"Hurry back, I'm first on your dance card," the young Hershey gentleman said.

Bea walked briskly to the powder room, but changed her mind about resting. Instead, she searched for Grandpa Bart. She needed answers and prayed to convince him to give them to her. So many things nagged at her—*How did she really lose her memory? What was really destined to happen on her sixteenth birthday? How did she prophesize the Titanic sinking? Or did she hear it from someone? And why did she spin a tale to Shirley about meeting a mermaid?*

Chapter Thirty-One

"Grandpa Bart!" Bea hollered on the stone terrace. Just as she'd expected, he'd snuck a cigar. Grandma Olivia would kill him is she'd found him smoking.

"Bea? What is it?" He quickly extinguished his cigar on the stone balcony with a guilty expression.

"Grandpa, we talked about this!" Bea put her hands on her hips and leaned forward with the same stern expression she'd inherited from her grandmother.

"Don't tell Olivia, she'd beat me 'til I bled." Grandpa drained his brandy tumbler.

"I won't tell her, *if* you'll tell me what everyone is hiding," Bea bargained with her arms crossed.

"Uh, let's go inside before Olivia sees me out here and smells the nasty cigar smoke." Grandpa's eyes darted with paranoia.

They meandered through the vast rooms downstairs, attempting to find one void of guests and servants. Settling in a quiet corner by the atrium, they sat in two cozy chairs.

"Spill it," Bea ordered.

"What?"

"I know ya'll are keeping a huge secret from me. Something about how I really lost my memory. Your lies don't match. Dad says I fell out of a tree in the *back*yard, you said it was the *front*."

Grandpa looked up with a quizzical expression, then twirled his silver beard with his index finger. "Ya know my memory isn't what it used to be."

"See, there, I know you're lying because you always twirl your beard when you're lying." Bea pointed.

"I can't tell you, Baby Bea. We all promised." Grandpa dropped his chin and kicked the chair like a truant toddler aching to misbehave.

"Tell me what? I know you want to. It's my parents and Grandma that swore you to secrecy," Bea cajoled.

"I...." pausing, his expression grew shocked, and his eyes widened with incredulity.

"What, Grandpa? What happened? How bad could it be?" she asked.

Pointing, he opened his mouth, but couldn't get the words out.

Turning to the direction of his pointed finger, Bea scrambled to see what shocked him. All she saw was the atrium. It was beautiful, she credited, but not shocking. Exotic plants filled the glass atrium. A small waterfall drizzled water onto the stone below. Statues of mermaids scattered the tiny paradise. Tropical plants grew in large pots. One in particular, grew out of a beautiful silver bowl with intricate carvings on the rim and handles.

"Bea, try to remember." Grandpa begged, holding his hands in mock prayer.

"What am I looking at? I see lots of tropical plants, statues of mermaids, and a big silver bowl."

"It's not a *bowl*, and it's not *silver*. Come on, remember the *Book of Cauldrons*? Remember the mermaids?" Grandpa pleaded.

Bea's eyes volleyed between the mermaid statues and silver bowl, which wasn't really a silver bowl. Her mind envisioned the *Book of Cauldrons* and all its tales. It wasn't a bowl, it was a cauldron, and it wasn't silver, it was chromium.

"A Chromium Cauldron!" Bea pointed, her tone rang with excitement.

"Yes, good girl. Remember the legend of the Chromium Cauldron, think, Baby Bea." Grandpa's eyes filled with excitement and he scooted to the edge of his seat.

Studying the mermaid statue, her mind ached to recall the connection. Envisioning the *Book of Cauldrons*, she remembered the legend involved mermaids. She'd seen a Chromium Cauldron before, but not here, and not at home. *Then where?*

"I've seen one before, but not here. Grandpa, why can't I remember? Tell me!" she begged.

"Think Baby Bea. You're remembering. You're almost there," he pleaded.

Bea's mind flooded with memories—the Chromium Cauldron, Whitehall, the beach, the ocean, the mermaids, the sea sprites, Atlantis.

She clutched her hand over her heart and screamed, "Peter!"

Chapter Thirty-Two

"Oh, Baby Bea, you remember!" Grandpa Bart hugged her.

"I must go to him! Do I take this one? Or do I need to get the same one he presented me ten years ago?" Bea's mind raced with questions and memories. Although angered that they kept this from her for ten years, she'd interrogate them later. Now she must go to Peter—her true love!

"I think you must use the one he gave you. But first, we must get the spell book and potion ingredients from home." Bart studied the atrium with a quizzical expression.

"My parents."

"Olivia. We'll have to sneak away, they'll never let us go to Atlantis. But we won't tell them," he reasoned.

"But won't they worry? Like last time?" Bea asked.

Grandpa's eyes brightened. "I have an idea, come on." He grabbed her hand and led her up the stone circular staircase to his room. He unlocked the door, entered the dimly lit room, and rummaged through his trunk.

Bea studied him. "What do you have in mind, Grandpa?"

Grandpa retrieved a small vial of liquid and held it up. "Aha, a sleeping potion, we'll slip this into their drinks, then slip away for a day. They'll never know we were even gone." He beamed.

"Genius." Bea smiled excitedly. Although remorseful about drugging her parents and grandma, she justified it with the fact that they somehow kept her memories suppressed for ten years.

"Come on. Don't act too excited, we can't let on that you regained your memory," Grandpa ordered.

"You, too, Grandpa. You're acting like a giddy school boy," Bea teased.

They walked back downstairs and were greeted by Olivia, Violet, and Toliver.

"There you two are. We've been searching for you everywhere. Why do you look like you're hiding something?" Olivia asked intuitively.

Bea and Grandpa exchanged worrisome expressions.

Then Grandpa's eye lit up. "Well, you caught us. Bea was just telling me about an extraordinary young man. Let's toast. I'll get some champagne." Bart excused himself.

"I'll help, Grandpa." Bea placed her hand in the crook of Grandpa's elbow. Once they were out of hearing range, she whispered, "Nice save, Grandpa."

They found a butler's pantry and helped themselves to a bottle of champagne and five Waterford Crystal flutes. Grandpa poured three glasses nearly to the rim and two only halfway. He retrieved the glass vial from his tuxedo jacket pocket and added one drop of the sleeping potion into the three full champagne flutes.

"Why do I feel guilty?" Bea asked.

"Because you're a good witch." Grandpa winked. "There, one drop equals one day of sleep."

"How quickly will it hit them?" Bea envisioned her parents and grandmother passing out the instant the sleeping potion touched their lips.

"Pretty quickly, but not too fast. By the time they finish their champagne, they'll grow tired. We'll suggest that we all call it a night. Once they're sound asleep in their beds, meet me back by the atrium," Grandpa explained.

"Ah, what took you so long?" Violet asked, taking one of the full flutes.

Just as they'd hoped.

Bart handed Olivia and Toliver the other two full glasses of champagne.

Bea held one of the half-filled flutes, then raised it and toasted. "To my future husband."

Chapter Thirty-Three

"Ready?" Grandpa Bart asked Bea. They stood by the atrium with the mermaid statues and Chromium Cauldron.

Nodding, Bea took Grandpa's hand and chanted, "*Eo Ire Itum*, Manchester Mansion attic, New Orleans." Traditionally, the eldest Manchester in the traveling group chanted the magic words, like a nod of respect to one's elders. But Grandpa, always spoiling her, let her cast the travelling spell.

Bea closed her eyes, like she always did when she traveled magically. By the time she opened them, they were back home in the attic. Shaking her legs, she mitigated the travel cramps which often accompanied *Eo Ire Itum*.

Grandpa retrieved the *Book of Cauldrons*, blew the dust off, and handed it to her.

Taking the book, she sat in one of the gold wing-back chairs. Waving her fingers, she magically started a fire. Shuddering, she asked. "Why am I getting déjà vu?"

"It's not déjà vu, you've done this before." Grandpa smiled with pride.

More memories flooded her mind. "That was my first power, wasn't it?" she asked, incredulous that after ten years of no memories before she was six, she now recalled the first time she magically started a fire like it was yesterday.

Beaming, he nodded. "My pride and joy, Baby Bea."

Opening the *Book of Cauldrons*, her fingers quickly found the page with the Chromium Cauldron spell. "I remember, you read me the legends from these books like they were bedtime stories."

"We did that after you lost your memory, too. But yes, I started our tradition when you were a baby. You didn't understand anything, but you liked the sound of my voice and the routine of hearing me read to you before bedtime." Grandpa searched the bookshelves.

"Grandpa, can you please get me an ink quill and parchment?" she asked. "I need to write this spell down to take with us to Palm Beach."

"Where did I put it?" Grandpa searched.

Pointing, she said, "The parchment and ink quill are on the desk."

He opened a small drawer. "Ah, here it is. I took this from you when you lost your memory." He handed her an aged piece of parchment.

"What's this?" Bea unfolded the parchment. Taken aback, she stared at the incantation and potion ingredients to cast the Chromium Cauldron spell. But what shocked her more than the word themselves, was that the words were written in *her* handwriting.

"For some reason, I wanted to save this. I hid it from everyone for ten years," he confessed.

"That's right, I remember now. You and I came home from Whitehall to get the spell after I met Peter on the beach," she recalled.

"Yes, Bea. Your memories are returning as quickly as they disappeared."

"We'll discuss *that* later," she quipped. Studying the potion ingredients, the words *dragon shrooms* piqued her curiosity. Looking up to the potion shelf, she recalled the abundance of rare shrooms her parents hoarded for over ten years. "That's why we have so much dragon shrooms."

"Yes, we knew one day you'd be reunited with Prince Peter. We asked our Manchester cousins in Scotland to harvest as much as possible with their fire breathing dragon."

"That's right, I'm supposed to marry him on my sixteenth birthday, that's two weeks away." Bea clutched her hand to her chest, and her heart longed to be with her true love again.

Grandpa grabbed all the potion ingredients and stuffed them into his knapsack. "I think I got everything."

Meow. Penelope slinked into the attic, obviously hearing the commotion, and jumped onto Bea's lap.

"Hello, sweet baby. Did you miss me?" she asked.

Purring, Penelope circled, lay down, and closed her eyes.

Recalling the tale spun about how she lost her memory falling from a tree while attempting to rescue her then kitten, Penelope, she asked, "Now, out with it. How did I really lose my memory?"

Dropping his shoulders defeatedly, Grandpa sighed. "Your grandmother erased your memory."

"What? How could she?" Horror shot through her.

"To save your life," Grandpa explained everything including her not eating for days and nearly wasting away to nothing.

"Remind me to thank her later for saving my life. But now it is time to begin the rest of mine." Standing, she took Grandpa's hand and chanted, "*Eo Ire Itum*, Whitehall, Palm Beach."

Chapter Thirty-Four

Bea and Grandpa Bart appeared in the opulent dining room of Whitehall. Luckily it was summer so the Flaglers were not in residence. Whitehall was merely their winter home.

The Chromium Cauldron resided against the side wall of the dining room, just as she remembered. Incredulous, Bea couldn't fathom that the Flaglers and their guests used it to hold wine.

"There it is." Grandpa smiled.

Picking it up, the weight surprised her. "I'd forgotten how heavy it was. But I was five when I last touched it."

"Here, I'll carry it for you." Grandpa took the cauldron from Bea. He carried the cauldron through the music room, into the enormous foyer, and to the front door.

Opening the door for him, guilt rushed through her and she asked, "Why do I feel like I'm stealing?"

"Because we are, my dear," he laughed.

Walking in silence, they traversed the dirt path to the beach. Passing the tall cypress trees on the way, Bea recalled climbing one when she first saw Peter doing flips in the ocean. Excitement filled her. This was really happening—she was going to see her destiny today!

"Are you excited or nervous?" Grandpa turned to her.

"Yes." Now apprehension took over. *What if she couldn't find him? What if he'd forgotten her? What if he didn't love her anymore? What if he was mad because she didn't visit him for the last ten years? Or worse, what if he loved someone else?*

"Don't fret, my dear. Peter will still remember and love you. You're destined to be together. I think that's why your memories returned. True love broke the memory spell your grandmother cast to save your life," he speculated.

"My feelings are torn about her erasing my precious memories of Peter, the mermaids, and Atlantis. But even more angry that many of my childhood memories were deleted, too. Who does that?" Anger boiled through her.

"I understand your anger. That was a horrible thing to do. But we were all at our wits' end. You were devastatingly broken hearted about Peter. You refused to eat or drink. You completely lost the will to live. We even gave you Penelope as a kitten. That did nothing to lift your spirits. Erasing your memories was our only hope. If you couldn't remember why you were sad, then you wouldn't be sad," he rationalized.

They arrived at the beach and walked on the same rocks which jettied out into the ocean.

"Well, there's no sense dwelling on the past. My future is with Peter," Bea reasoned optimistically.

"That's my girl." Grandpa set the cauldron down on a flat rock, then removed the knapsack from his shoulder and handed it to Bea.

Bea dipped the Chromium Cauldron into the water and filled it partway. Then she added the ingredients, grateful that her family hoarded dragon shrooms these last ten years. She chanted the magical words to cast the Chromium Cauldron spell. Then she drank the potion.

"Don't forget to test it first," he reminded her.

"Of course. Where should I return to after my twenty-four hours are up?" she asked.

"Just go straight to the Biltmore. I will meet you there. Then we'll explain everything to Violet, Toliver, and Oliva," he said.

"Then we can plan my wedding." Bea winked.

"That's my girl, think happy thoughts." He hugged her goodbye.

Bea stepped into the sea, and let the waves splash over her. Grateful for the warm summer water, she submerged. Opening her eyes, the clear and calm green-blue water offered great visibility. She opened her mouth and let the salt water in. Gagging reflexively, she let the water fill her mouth and lungs, then breathed underwater.

Grandpa studied her underwater.

She nodded, gave him a thumbs up, and smiled. Then she chanted, *"Eo Ire Itum, Atlantis."*

Chapter Thirty-Five

Bea opened her eyes underwater and the breathtaking view of Atlantis surrounded her. Smiling, she searched for her beloved—Prince Peter the merman.

Mermaids swam through the water with great speed. Some lounged on the ocean floor, oblivious to the human intruder. The golden columns of the palace glistened from the strange light source radiating from the bottom of the sea.

Bea swam to the palace and entered through an arched window. The throne room was just as she remembered, only King Triton, Peter's father, was not on the throne. The palace was empty, and Bea had no idea where to search for her true love. Precious minutes wasted away.

"Excuse me. What are you doing here?" a merman guard asked. His gaze dropped to the Chromium Cauldron she held. Luckily, it blocked the view of her legs. Mermaids hated and feared humans.

"Oh, sorry. I'm looking for Prince Peter." She prayed he was alive and well, but missing her as much as she missed him.

"Is he expecting you?" the guard asked, grasping his spear protectively.

"He'll be thrilled to see me." Bea spoke the truth while evading the question.

"Peter, thrilled? He hasn't been thrilled for the last ten years. He kept escaping to the surface to see some human, and the King feared for his safety. King Triton forbade him from leaving the palace. But you should know all of this. It's the talk of the Atlantic," the guard explained.

Trusting this guard, Bea boldly raised the cauldron and revealed her legs. "I'm the human he's been trying to see."

Gasping, the guard pointed the spear at her chest. "Don't come any closer. Who are you and how are you breathing underwater? What trickery is this?"

Bea stared into the merman's eyes, mesmerizing him with her spellbinding allure. "I'm his true love. I haven't seen him in ten years because I lost my memory. Ask the sea sprites if you don't believe me. But please, I'm begging you, take me to Peter!"

With a void expression, the guard nodded. The mesmerizing spell obviously worked. "Follow me," he said. The guard swam through several corridors and arrived at a closed door. "In there." Then he left her.

Bea turned the door handle. It was locked. Remembering her powers, she waved her hand and envisioned the door opening. It did.

Peter lay on the stone floor with his eyes closed. More handsome than she remembered, he'd grown into a man. His blond hair floated above his beautiful face. The scales of his teal fin reflected the light filtering in from the window.

He slept so peacefully that part of her didn't wish to disturb him. Staring at his handsome form, she savored this moment of their imminent reunion.

His body shook, yet he remained asleep. He mumbled a bunch of nonsense while tossing and turning on the stone floor. "Father, no! You can't keep me prisoner forever. I will escape your imprisonment, somehow, and find my true love."

Gasping, Bea realized that Peter was having a nightmare. She longed to wake him, but felt superstitious about disrupting the dream world.

"Beatrice! I miss you terribly. Please come back to me," he hollered in his sleep. His fin flapped repeatedly and banged against the stone floor.

"Peter, I'm here," Bea whispered and gently kissed his lips.

His eyes fluttered open, and he smiled. "Beatrice, my love. Am I dreaming? Am I in heaven?"

Chapter Thirty-Six

"Peter, I'm here. I'm finally here again!" Bea squealed with euphoria.

Sitting up, Peter blinked his eyes to ascertain if she was real. "Beatrice, I must be in heaven if you're with me. You're so beautiful." Peter took each of her hands and kissed them.

Blushing, Bea said, "You are very handsome, too."

They both rose, still holding hands, and admired one another. They'd both changed in the last ten years.

Peter cupped her face with each of his hands, looked lovingly and longingly into her eyes and said, "Oh, Bea. I've missed you." Then he kissed her. But not an innocent peck on the lips like when they were children. This kiss was passionate. Their tongues touched and souls reunited.

"Oh, Peter. I'm sorry I couldn't get here sooner. My parents erased my memory, and true love just returned it a few hours ago," Bea explained her absence.

"We're together now. Do you remember our vow?" He held her in his arms.

Nodding, she smiled.

"Let me do this right." Peter swam to a trunk, retrieved a small box, and presented it to her. "Beatrice Manchester, will you marry me?" He opened the box to reveal a beautiful ring with pearls.

Euphoric, she said, "Yes, Peter. I will marry you." She took the offered ring. Two pearls, one black and one opaque, rested in a setting on top of a gold ring. "It's a beautiful ring."

Placing it on her finger, her said, "Two different pearls representing two different species, uniting as one."

The water churned slightly nearby. A flapping sound resonated through the water like a sonar ping. Bea recognized the noise and turned to the window. Ella, Della, and Ida, the sea sprites, swam towards them with gleeful expressions.

"I told you. I sensed that true love was here," Ida swam excitedly, too.

"Ella, Della, and Ida," Bea greeted the sea sprites.

"Beatrice, Your Royal Highness." The sprites bowed reverently.

"Ella, Della, and Ida." Peter gestured for them to rise.

"Congratulations on your engagement. Bea, your sixteenth birthday is only two weeks away. There's much to do to plan the wedding—a Royal wedding. Bea, you'll be a Princess!" Ida fluttered around with the others, all elated about their prophecy's imminent fruition.

"A princess, oh my." Bea had never comprehended the title before. Questions of logistics swam in her mind. *Where would they live? Where would they get married. Would her parents attend the wedding?*

Peter squeezed her hand, like he intuitively knew her dilemma. "We'll figure it all out, my love. But no matter where we live or get married, we'll always be together." He kissed her.

"Oh dear. I almost forgot. We have some scary news." Ella's expression grew dim.

"The Gods are angry again. The humans are building these beautiful mansions along the seashore, flaunting their wealth and prosperity in Poseidon's face," Della said.

Bea immediately thought about the beautiful homes and opulent hotels she'd visited over the years—Ponce De Leon, Alcazar, Royal Poinciana, Breakers, Whitehall, and most recently, the Biltmore.

"Oh no. What do they plan to do? Sink another luxury ocean liner?" Bea asked, remembering the Titanic.

"I wish it was only another sinking ship. Poseidon, using his powerful Trident, plans to generate the biggest hurricane of all time and destroy Florida."

Chapter Thirty-Seven

"*Eo Ire Itum*, Biltmore Estate, North Carolina," Bea chanted.

Instantaneously arriving at the beautiful estate, Bea quickly sought out her Grandpa Bart. Luckily, she found them all having tea in a common living room near their guest rooms. "I have so much to tell you, all of you."

"Ah, there you are. I'm afraid we all slept in quite a bit. We woke up in time for tea, at least." Toliver put the newspaper down, stood, and kissed the top of her head. "I was just about to read the paper."

Frantic, Bea read the date on the paper. Knowing it was a day later, Bea shot Grandpa Bart a worried stare.

Grandpa took the hint, and discreetly removed the paper from the coffee table. As he slid it under a cushion, Bea glimpsed the paper's headline— Hurricane destroys islands east of the Caribbean. *The sea sprites were right!*

Scanning the room, Bea searched for strangers. Luckily, they were all alone, and it was safe to explain the twenty-four hours.

"Baby Bea? What's wrong, you look like the proverbial cat who swallowed the canary," Violet chuckled.

"I have so much to tell you, but I'm not sure where to start." Bea glanced at Grandpa for guidance.

Nodding at her to continue, Grandpa Bart said, "Just start from the beginning."

Drawing a big breath, she spewed out the highlights. "My memory returned. I went to see Prince Peter in Atlantis. He proposed, and I said yes." Pausing, she held out her ringed finger for everyone to admire. "We are to be married on my sixteenth birthday, just like the sea sprites prophesized."

"Oh, my, Baby Bea." Dad hugged her, then everyone else joined in.

"I'm so happy for you. How did your memory return?" Mom asked, shooting Grandpa Bart a dirty look.

"I saw a Chromium Cauldron in the Biltmore's atrium downstairs. My memories simply flooded back to me. Then I gathered the potion ingredients and spell incantation, took *my* Chromium Cauldron back from the Flaglers at Whitehall, cast the spell, then returned to Atlantis," Bea summarized in one breath.

"There's so much to do. We have less than two weeks. I assume the wedding will be in Atlantis. It's not every day the prince of Atlantis marries a human." Mom dove right into the wedding planning.

Olivia piped in, "I'll find a spell which will allow us to breathe underwater so we can attend the wedding." Touching her index finger to her temple, she added, "I think there is a bubble spell. We can make the bubble big enough for all of us to breathe in during the ceremony."

"Luckily, your father and I hoarded enough dragon shrooms for you to breathe underwater for the rest of your life," Mom boasted.

"We'll have to find a spell for Peter to come on land. Perhaps you can spend half of your time with us, and the other in Atlantis." Dad rubbed his goatee with his thumb and index finger.

"Check with the Elders in Scotland. King Triton told me that Mordecai Manchester conjured such a spell when he married King Triton's royal ancestor. He told me about it when I visited Atlantis the first time." Excitement and hope consumed Bea. She fantasized about Peter walking on land with her.

100

Mom's face lit up. "I just realized, our Baby Bea will be a Princess of Atlantis." Mom hugged her again. The rest of her family joined together in another emotional group hug.

Remembering the hurricane, Bea gasped. "The Gods are angry at the humans again. Poseidon generated a giant hurricane. The fairies said it was big enough to destroy the entire state of Florida."

"That's insanity," Olivia quipped.

"Remember the Titanic? They knew it would sink, but nobody believed us."

"Ah, she's right." Toliver nodded.

Bea grabbed the newspaper and showed it to her family. "See!"

"Oh, my. But what can we do?" Dad asked.

"Many of the Manchesters can control the weather. Perhaps they can stop it," Olivia suggested.

"I guess we're all going to Scotland to gather the coven," Grandpa Bart said.

Dad snatched the newspaper from Bea. "Let me see that. Why is the paper dated tomorrow?" Toliver asked.

"Must be a misprint, some of those newsies are imbeciles." Grandpa winked at Bea.

Chapter Thirty-Eight

All holding hands in a circle, Bart chanted, *"Eo Ire Itum,* Manchester Manor, Isle of Skye, Scotland."

The American Manchesters instantly appeared in the formal parlor room of Manchester Manor. Luckily, many were still awake and enjoying brandy and cigars.

Startled, Bart's mother shrieked with excitement. "Bart, Olivia, oh my, what a pleasant surprise. I was just complaining to your aunts and uncles that you don't visit your aging mother enough."

All the Manchesters hugged in reunion. "Mom, there's no time to explain. Please, gather the Elders and all Manchesters with the power to control the weather."

Bart's mother closed her eyes. Using her power of telepathy, she summoned the Elders and weather-controlling Manchesters.

Manchesters popped into the formal parlor one by one. The room quickly filled with at least fifty Manchesters who squeezed together in the diminishing space.

Grandpa Bart stood on a chair and addressed the Manchester coven, "My fellow Manchesters, please forgive the short notice, but we have a crisis threatening to destroy many Americans. Your young, American Manchester cousin Beatrice will explain."

Bart grabbed Bea's hand and helped her up onto a mahogany Chippendale chair.

"My fellow Manchesters. Poseidon is furious with the humans again. He's generated the largest hurricane ever which will destroy all the Caribbean islands and the State of Florida. Millions will perish if we don't do something. That's why we summoned those with weather controlling powers," Bea explained.

"I know, since hurricanes spin *counterclockwise*, we can generate a giant water spout spinning *clockwise* to stop it," a Manchester witch suggested.

"If hurricanes thrive in warm water, we can freeze the water to stop its power source," a Manchester wizard said.

"But that'll freeze the sea creatures," another Manchester countered.

"We could levitate the hurricane into the air and throw the whole monstrosity into outer space," another Manchester offered an alternative solution.

"We could steer it away from land and send it up the middle of the Atlantic," another Manchester said.

"Those are all great ideas, but we still have a huge problem. How are we going to fly over the hurricane to stop it?" Bea asked.

"We need an angel!"

"More than that, we need *the* angel."

"As in..." Bea paused.

"St. Michael the Archangel."

"*Eo Ire Itum*, St. Michael's Church, Isle of Skye," the eldest Manchester chanted.

The Manchester coven instantly transported to the closest of St. Michael's numerous churches around the world.

The Manchesters all knelt and recited the prayer to summon their angel.

"Saint Michael the Archangel, defend us in battle; be our protection against the wickedness and snares of the devil, May God rebuke him, we humbly pray: and do thou, O Prince of the heavenly host, by the power of God, thrust into hell Satan, and all the evil spirits who prowl about the world seeking the ruin of souls. Amen."

Chapter Thirty-Nine

A flapping noise echoed throughout the church. In front of the stained-glass window depicting St. Michael the Archangel, *he* appeared.

Bea gasped, along with the rest of her coven. Before them stood the most magnificent and beautiful creature she'd ever seen. Aside from her handsome Prince Peter the merman, of course.

Golden curly ringlets framed Michael's pale, cherub face. Eyes, one blue and one green, matched her own. Lean muscles rippled his body. But the most magnificent feature of all were beautiful, white wings with gold tips. His wings spanned nearly ten feet, stretching the length of the marble altar.

"Hello, my descendants." Michael smiled.

Bea had forgotten the legend that he was her ancestor. In 1592, Michael took the human form for two reasons—to fight the giant evil in the forest and to be reunited with his soul mate, her ancestor, Prudence Manchester Garrison, Countess of Garrison.

An elder Manchester, Eleanor, stood and bowed. "Dearest Michael, thank you for coming so quickly. We are truly honored by your presence."

"I always come when you say my prayer in one of my churches. How may I help my children?"

Eleanor explained the massive hurricane threatening millions of humans.

"How many of you have the power to control the weather?" Michael asked.

More than two dozen Manchester wizards and witches raised their hands, including Bea.

"We're going to need more wings." Michael sang in Latin. Angelic words poured from his lips.

Two dozen angels flew into the church and landed next to Michael in front of the altar.

"If you can control the weather, please step forward and pair with an angel to fly you over the hurricane and create water spouts spinning clockwise."

Bea rose and ascended three marble steps to the altar. Studying all the angels, she wasn't sure which one to pick. She weighed ninety pounds soaking wet, so the angel needn't be particularly strong, but they all were. Then one picked her.

Turning, Bea gasped.

St. Michael himself stood majestically in front of her. "Hello, Beatrice." Michael extended his hand to shake.

Startled, Bea shook his hand and said, "It's nice to meet you."

A bolt struck through her hand the instant she touched his.

"Whoa! Did you feel that?" Michael asked.

"Yes, what was that? It felt like electricity ran through my hand." Bea shuddered.

"But not our hearts, darn." Michael snapped his fingers with disappointment.

"What are you talking about?" Bea feared she'd somehow disappointed him.

"I'm sure you've heard the legend. My reincarnated soul mate, a Manchester witch with magical eyes, will be born in the New World before the end of *this* millennia."

Gasping, she said, "That's still nearly eighty years away. But I was born in the New World and I have magical eyes. Did you think that I... could be your soulmate?"

"I'd hoped. But if you were, my heart would know instantly. You can imagine how excited I am to spend another mortal lifetime on earth with my beloved. It's been over three centuries."

"I'm sorry, I'm not her. Besides, my soul mate is Prince Peter of Atlantis. We are to marry on my sixteenth birthday in less than two weeks," Bea beamed.

"What a lucky merman. But there is something drawing me to you. It's not true love, but some sort of adoration." He placed his hand over her belly.

Giggling, she laughed, "That tickles."

"Perhaps you will be the mortal mother of my soulmate, or even her grandmother. Please, I'm begging you, hurry up and procreate," Michael pleaded.

Gasping, the realization sank in. "That means, I'll be able to successfully mate with my true love. King Triton wasn't sure since this is the first time a mer*man* has mated with a female human."

"My bride will be part mermaid, interesting," Michael contemplated.

"Wouldn't it be neat if your offspring have wings *and* a fin?"

"I'm thinking you will be her grandmother, if my soulmate were to be the fruit of thy womb, I'd feel it." Michael sighed.

"You should come to my wedding. It'll be in Atlantis." Bea invited her first guest.

"I'd be honored to be at the wedding of my soul mate's grandparents. Please tell your daughter or son to name your granddaughter a name which starts with the letter 'P', like Penelope. It's sort of our ongoing joke. We've used Persephone and Prudence," Michael requested.

Laughing she said, "Penelope is the name of my cat."

Chapter Forty

"Ahem," Grandpa Bart cleared his throat, interrupting the special moment between Bea and Michael.

"Oh, right. Angels and witches, assume your flying positions," Michael ordered. Standing behind Bea, Michael wrapped his arms around her waist. His warmth consumed her. "Hook your ankles with mine, and hold on tight."

Following the order, she secured herself as best she could. Incredulous, she couldn't believe she was about to fly with an angel, let alone *the* angel.

"You know where we're going, right," Michael whispered.

His hot breath chilled her, prickling her skin with goosebumps. Part of her envied her future granddaughter. "Eastern Caribbean."

Michael flapped his powerful wings, flew them out of the church, and up into the moonlit night. He paused, hovering above his church while the other angels flew out with their magical passengers.

Once all the angels hovered outside, Michael said, "Hold on tight because we're about to fly really fast."

Michael and the other angels sang in Latin. As their words accelerated, so did they. They flew extremely fast, making Bea nauseous. But the experience of flying with the angel who would marry her granddaughter filled her heart with bliss. She couldn't wait to add the tale to the *Book of Legends*.

The hurricane was easy to spot. Its massive width spanned over five hundred miles. From the sky, the hurricane resembled an enormous pinwheel, slowly rotating counterclockwise. At the center of the gigantic hurricane was an immense eye, many miles wide. Peering down through the eye, the ocean's surface resided below. She prayed Peter and all the mermaids were safe. The northwest quadrant of the storm hadn't hit Cuba yet where Atlantis rested just below its surface.

Michael pointed, "That's the eye of the hurricane, it's deceivingly calm. But the most powerful part of the hurricane is the eye wall. This one is the windiest and biggest I've ever encountered. Poseidon is really mad at the humans. These winds are gusting over two hundred miles an hour."

Wind blew through Bea's hair and stung her face.

"Everyone, remember the plan. Let's spread out around the eye wall and form your waterspouts clockwise," Michael commanded.

Bea waved her hand clockwise and willed the air to spin. A tiny tornado formed, spiraling beautifully.

All the other Manchesters did the same thing. Two dozen tornadoes formed above the hurricane, equally spaced along the circumference of the eye wall.

Widening her reach, she envisioned it growing wider and taller. Once it was a full tornado, she forced it down through the eye wall. The other two dozen tornados entered the eye, and descended through its calm center to the ocean's surface.

Once Bea's tornado reached the surface, it became a water spout spinning in the opposite direction of the hurricane. Then she waved her hand towards her, pulling her water spout into the eye wall.

The other witches and wizards did the same thing.

Like a cog in a wheel, the force of the water spouts in the opposite direction stalled the hurricane. The enormous pinwheel stopped, the eyewall vanished, and the clouds dissipated. The winds stopped, and the sea below grew calm. They did it! They destroyed the hurricane!

"Yippee!" Bea squealed. Pride enveloped her. They'd saved millions of lives—on land *and* in the sea.

Chapter Forty-One

Two weeks later
Atlantis

Bea floated in the ancient church in Atlantis. Her black hair, up in a bun, was secured with a pearl tiara. Her white dress, made special for her, was the most beautiful silk dress she'd ever seen. Simple in design, but elegant in its details, the dress was conjured by the sea sprites. A long lace train floated elegantly behind her.

Hundreds of mermaids lined the long aisle leading to the altar. Her mother and grandparents, all inside a giant air bubble, floated close to the altar. King Triton floated on the opposite side of the aisle from her family wearing his crown and holding his scepter majestically. Michael, floated angelically above the altar with his beautiful wings fully extended.

But the most beautiful sight before her was her Prince, her destiny, her true love—Peter the merman. He wore a white shirt which clung to his muscular torso. His teal fin flapped gently, floating him in front of the altar.

Luckily, the Manchesters had studied the ancient scrolls and found the spell Mordecai Manchester had used on his mermaid wife centuries ago. This spell allowed Peter to have legs when he was on land. And with Bea's unlimited supply of dragon shrooms, she could easily breathe underwater in Atlantis. They planned to split their time between the Manchester Mansion in New Orleans, and the beautiful golden palace in Atlantis. Once they had a baby, their permanent home would depend on whether or not the fruit of their love had a fin!

A team of large seahorses pulled a chariot through the water, escorting Bea down the aisle. Her doting father, Toliver, floated in his own bubble next to Bea. The seahorses pulled her to Peter—her destiny, her true love.

Arriving at the front of the church, Bea exited the chariot. Her father blew her a kiss and presented her to Peter.

Peter lifted the veil from her face, then pulled it over her tiara. Taking her hand, he smiled. Together, they turned to face St. Michael the Archangel, who greeted them with a wink.

"Dearly beloved."

The End

Epilogue

Seven years later
October 24, 1929
Mount Olympus

"What is wrong, Zeus?" Athena, the Goddess of Wisdom asked.

"It's those pesky mortals. I tried to teach them a lesson and make them humble before me, but our plan failed. Poseidon created a hurricane to destroy their beautiful homes along the beaches of Florida, but those pesky witches teamed up with the mermaids and angels and stopped the storm. Each time we generate one, the witches either weakens it, or redirects it away from land."

"I have an idea. If we can't destroy their homes, perhaps we can destroy their vast wealth," Athena turned to Zeus to gauge his reaction.

"Interesting, how do we destroy their wealth?" Zeus asked.

"I've studied the wealthy mortals and their financial economy. It's complicated, but it can be done." Athena grinned wickedly, "I'll ruin the banks, crash the stock market, and create a Great Depression."

Excerpt from

Copper Cauldron

Prologue

"Can you tell me a bedtime story, Great-Grandma?" Penelope asked.

The nine-year old girl looked at her great-grandmother whose eyes matched her own, one blue and one green. She lay in her pink bedroom on the second floor of the ancestral mansion located in the Garden District of New Orleans. Penelope, born in this house, represented the seventh generation of Manchester Witches to live here.

"Of course, my dear. Which story would you like to hear? Or do I even need to ask?" Violet said, smiling.

"You know the one, my favorite," Penelope answered. She laid her small head down. Her long black hair spread across the pillow.

"I love this story too. Once upon a time, there was a young woman named Penelope. Her beautiful long black hair hung to her tiny waist. Her pale skin gave her a beautiful, youthful complexion. She possessed the most unique and treasured eyes, one blue and one green. One day, she will meet her one true love, her soul mate, her destiny. He is a warrior of God, with the face of an angel, the heart of a saint, and eyes which match her own," Violet said.

"Thank you, Great-Grandma. When are Ma and Da coming home?" Penelope asked.

"Your parents are busy fighting bad people. I hope they'll be home very soon."

"Why didn't Grandma Beatrice go with them this time?" Penelope asked.

"Beatrice wanted to stay behind and keep an eye

on us," Violet replied.

"Why do we have to keep our powers a secret?" Penelope asked.

"Because it scares people," Violet said.

"Am I really the youngest Manchester Witch to receive her powers?" Penelope asked.

"Yes, you are. You will be a very powerful and very good witch. It is part of your destiny. Your true love will be very powerful, too. But your children will be even more powerful than you," Violet explained.

"When can we go see another Church of St. Michael?" Penelope asked. She looked over at the wall behind her great-grandmother. She stared at the painting of St. Michael the Archangel, her family's patron saint.

"We just went to the one in Charleston. How many St. Michael's churches do you want to visit?" Violet asked.

"I want to go to all of them."

"What is your infatuation with St. Michael the Archangel?" Violet asked.

"He's the one I'm going to marry. He is my destiny," Penelope said, smiling as she closed her eyes and drifted off to sleep.

Excerpt from

Cobalt Cauldron

Chapter One

1894 Egypt

"Ma, I'm getting dirty." Violet Manchester pouted.
The six-year-old accompanied her parents on a dig in
Egypt, and everything Egyptian fascinated her.

"Today is our last day digging in Luxor. Next, we'll
go to the museum in Cairo." Bartholomew, Bart for
short, held his daughter's hand. "You're being a very
good girl."

"Thank you, Da." Staring at her father's adoring
face, capped with long blond hair, she admired his
magical eyes—one green and one blue.

Violet inherited the Manchester family trait of
magical eyes. She inherited her long black hair and
ivory complexion from her mother. But she'd yet to
come into her powers of witchcraft.

"That's my big girl." Picking her up, he placed her
on his hip. "What's your favorite part about Egypt?"

Basking in her Da's attention, she contemplated
his question with her index finger touching her chin.
"Hmmmm, the pyramids and the Sphinx."

"Those were my favorite things, too. But we'll see
some cool stuff tomorrow, like mummies."

Violet fainted, and a vision flashed through her
head.

*A gold mask with the image of a handsome boy
appeared. The gold mask was part of an ornate*

sarcophagus. A mummy was placed inside of it, and the room was surrounded with treasure. The walls were painted with pretty pictures, including two Egyptian figures. The burial chamber's entrance was sealed with stone doors covered in hieroglyphs. The vision of the tomb zoomed out to the surrounding landscape of the desert.

"Tutankhamun," she whispered.

"What's wrong with her? What happened?" Olivia, Violet's mother, wailed.

"I don't know. Her eyes went blank, and then she fainted." He knelt next to his little girl.

"Is it the heat? Give her some water." Olivia held her daughter's hand.

When Violet opened her eyes, her parents huddled above her with worried expressions. "Ma? Da?"

"Oh, thank God, Violet. You're awake." Her Da sighed.

Sitting up, she asked, "Who's Tutankhamun?"

"You mumbled his name. Tutankhamun was the Pharaoh of Egypt from 1332-1323 B.C. They called him King Tut for short. He ruled at the age of nine, but died when he was only eighteen. He married his half-sister when he was only nine." Da handed her a full canteen of water.

"Married at nine? I thought ladies weren't wed until fifteen?" She sat up and drank from the canteen.

"That's true now, but things were different three thousand years ago. Why did you say his name?" Picking her up, he plopped her on his lap like he was about to read her a bedtime story.

"I had a vision. I saw his tomb of a gold mask with blue stripes. It's beautiful." Violet wrapped her arms around her Da's neck.

"How do you know that? They've never found his

tomb."

Olivia held her hand to her throat and gasped, "Her powers! She must have the power of foresight."

"Of course, my mother had the same power. And you received it so young." Cooing, he hugged Violet.

While hugging her father, her gaze went to the same hill formation she saw in her vision. "We're digging in the wrong place. We need to dig over there." She pointed.

"Oh, honey. We're just digging for fun. It's how these Egyptian men make a living, taking wealthy adventurers on a dig. We never expected to find anything," Ma reasoned.

"But those hills. I saw them in my vision when I zoomed out of the tomb. That's where we need to dig." Standing on her tiny legs, she pointed. "Can we dig over there, Da? Pretty please?" She clasped her hands together, begging.

Smiling down at her he said, "Of course, my darling, Violet. Let's go dig over there."

Chapter Two

"Look, Da. It's the entrance to Tutankhamun's tomb." Violet pointed excitedly at the stone door they'd reached after only an hour of digging.

"How in the world are we supposed to move this stone door? It must weigh a ton." Da dropped his head, defeated.

"Bart, dear, remember *my* powers." Ma referred to her telekinetic powers. She moved her hand across the stone door, and it slowly opened with a loud scraping sound.

"Thank you, my dear. I'll go in first." Da lit his lantern and ducked into the tomb.

"Wait for me, Da." Violet picked up her lantern with one hand and grabbed her Da's hand with the other.

A room filled with treasure greeted them. Gold jewelry, cobalt jewelry, coins, plates, and pottery filled the room, all ready to follow King Tut into the afterlife, or so the Egyptians believed.

"Wow, this is amazing." Ma followed them into the tomb.

"Look at these paintings on the walls. They're exquisite." Bart held the lantern higher which illuminated the large drawings on the wall.

"I saw those in my vision." Violet sang and skipped around the tomb with glee. "I have my powers. I have my powers. I can see the future."

Stopping suddenly, her eyes focused on a beautiful cobalt cauldron. She was drawn to it. She'd never seen anything like it. Picking it up, she rubbed off over three millennia of dust. The brilliant cobalt-blue color mesmerized her. Although heavy in her tiny hands, it was smaller than the ones her parents kept in the attic. She was normally a good child, but a devious moment consumed her. She just had to have this cobalt cauldron. Now compulsion dictated her. While her parents studied the paintings on the walls, she slipped the cobalt cauldron into her knapsack.

"Where's the mummy?" Ma asked, scanning the room.

Violet pointed to a set of engraved doors like she saw in her vision. "He's in there. That's the burial chamber."

The trio stood in front of the shrine doors engraved with hieroglyphs. "Wait, what if it's cursed?" Ma stepped back.

"Remember *my* powers, my dear." He could reverse any curse or spell. Standing, he raised his hands above his head. Closing his eyes, he said, "I remove all curses and spells from this tomb of Tutankhamun, Pharaoh of Egypt."

"Now it's your turn, my dear." Da nodded towards the shrine doors.

Again, Ma waved her hand, and the stone doors opened at her nonverbal command.

"Me first, me first." Not waiting for permission, Violet walked through the opening holding the lantern above her head. The lantern illuminated the room, and a gold mask with King Tut's youthful image appeared.

"Hi, Tutankhamun. It's nice to meet you."

Another vision filled her.

The boy king's spirit floated above the cobalt cauldron. But not here in his Egyptian tomb, he floated above the cauldron in her room at their home in New Orleans.

"Violet? Are you alright?" Bart knelt next to her.

"Uh, huh. Da, this is King Tut." Pointing, she kept

her vision to herself.

"I see that. You were right, my dear. You've discovered his tomb."

"Are we rich now?" She grabbed her Da's hand.

"Violet, we're already rich because of the Manchester dynasty."

"Bart, dear. We can't keep this, any of it." Ma stood next to Da and admired the gold sarcophagus.

"I know. It belongs to the people of Egypt. Won't they be thrilled to have such a beautiful collection to add to their museum in Cairo?"

"We can't tell anyone. We can't disturb the dead, or let anyone else disturb it."

"Of course, my dear. Violet, take one last look at Tutankhamun."

She studied the ornate coffin. "Goodbye, King Tut." Smiling, she thought of her cobalt cauldron and her last vision. She'd see King Tut again.

"Perhaps a spell is in order, Bart. We should protect this from looters and grave robbers. The dead need to rest."

"Of course, my dear." Da raised his hands above his head and said, "Protect this tomb of Tutankhamun. I curse it with an early death to all who open it, hereafter."

They exited the tomb and outer chamber. Once outside, Ma waved her hands, and the stone door moved back into place. After walking over a mile away, Ma waved both hands. A sandstorm blew in and covered the tomb's entrance under a mountain of sand.

Chapter Three

"Da, why can't we take the boat back home?"

A few days later, Violet and her parents stood in their hotel room in Egypt, surrounded by their trunks.

"We're going to *Eo Ire Itum* home." Da picked her up.

Eo Ire Itum, Latin for 'to travel', referred to the instant travel method available to witches and wizards.

"Okay, Da. I like traveling that way. It's so fast."

"Me, too. Do we have everything?" he asked.

Violet nodded, thrilled to take her cobalt cauldron home with her. She couldn't wait to play with it. "Da, can I have a kitten when we get home?" she pleaded. Even at six, she knew her Da couldn't resist her magical eyes and innocent face. That's what Ma called, 'wrapping him around her little finger.'

"Of course, Violet. Anything for my, baby girl."

"Ready?"

Violet and Ma nodded.

Da chanted, "*Eo Ire Itum*. Manchester Mansion, New Orleans, Louisiana."

They arrived at their destination instantly—the attic of their mansion in the Garden District of New Orleans. The attic topped the three-story mansion, four including the basement. Plenty of room for more Manchester witches which often visited from their ancestral home in Scotland.

The dark and dusty room contained a round stained glass window overlooking the sidewalk leading to the house. The attic, with shelves lined with potions and cauldrons, was where her parents worked their magic. By the window stood a podium topped with their *Book of Spells*.

"Ah, it's great to be home." Ma shook her limbs and kicked her legs, shaking off the travel cramps which often accompanied *Eo Ire Itum*.

"Can I go play with my dolls in my room, Da?" she asked.

"Of course, my dear." He set her down.

Grabbing her knapsack, she ran towards the stairs. Turning she hollered, "Don't forget my kitten, Da. Promise?"

"I promise." He beamed.

She ran down the stairs to her pink bedroom on the second floor. Closing the door behind her, she plopped on her white canopied bed with a pink bedspread and matching curtains. Picking up her favorite doll, Anne, she hugged her close.

Remembering her cobalt cauldron, she jumped off the bed and sat on the rug between her bed and her window. If her parents came in, they wouldn't see her because the door was on the other side of the bed.

Removing her new treasure, she held the cauldron in her hand. "You're dirty. Let's give you a bath." Picking up a towel from her washing table, she dipped it into the white porcelain water bowl. Rubbing the wet towel along the side of the cauldron, she wiped it clean. Dipping the towel into the water again, she rubbed more dirt off the cauldron. After repeating the action three more times, she admired her clean, beautiful cobalt cauldron. The cobalt felt cool against her skin, and she hugged it close.

Thinking of Tutankhamun, it saddened her that he died so young. She wanted to talk to him and tell her how sorry she was. Remembering she had a power now, she wondered what else she could do. Her parents made magic look so easy. They simply waved their hands, and then said what magic they wanted. Sometimes they used the *Book of Spells*, but other times they didn't need to.

Placing the cauldron before her, she sat her doll against the wall to watch. "Want to talk to King Tut, Anne? Let's summon him."

Waving both hands over the cobalt cauldron, she said, "Tutankhamun, I, Violet Manchester, summon thee."

Closing her eyes, she waited. Squinting one eye open, she saw nothing. Disappointment filled her.

"Of course, I need a potion." She slid the cauldron under her bed and ran upstairs to the attic. Getting an empty soap box crate to stand on, she stepped up to the podium which displayed the *Book of Spells*. She turned the pages, grateful her parents taught her to read so young. A picture of a cobalt cauldron was painted into the left-hand side of the page. Drawings of Egyptians surrounded the cauldron. On the right side of the page, it read, "Talking to the dead."

The page listed the ingredients and words to invoke the spell. Violet quickly memorized the list and closed the spell book. Grabbing the ingredients from the shelf, she ran back downstairs to her room and closed the door.

Pulling the cobalt cauldron back out from under the bed, she dumped the ingredients into the cauldron, waved her hands over the potion, and recited the spell, "From beyond the grave, come to me now. Tutankhamun, I summon thee."

Excerpt from

Calcium Cauldron

"The battle against the devil, which is the principle task of St. Michael the archangel, is still being fought today because the devil is still alive and active in the world."

--Pope John Paul II

Prologue

"Michael, I have a special quest for you," God said.

"Yes, Father." Michael the Archangel bowed. His white wings with gold tips folded behind his back. Golden curly hair framed his handsome, cherub face.

"It is a very important, but a very long quest. You will be born again on earth. You will live the life of a mortal, but you will still have your powers."

"And my wings?" Michael looked up to God.

"Your wings will appear when you want them to. But you cannot reveal who you really are, except to your one true love."

"And what is my mission on this new path you have chosen for me?"

"You will battle evil in the Isle of Skye," God said.

Chapter One

January 1, 1600
Isle of Skye, Scotland

Prudence Manchester danced in the enchanted forest. Her long black hair fell to her waist. Her favorite pastime, dancing, coined her nickname—Dance. Her six-year-old body twirled under the nearly full moon. The morning hour marked the dawn of a new century—the 17th.

Many locals on the Isle of Skye were terrified to enter the enchanted forest. They referred to it as the forbidden forest. But Dance wasn't afraid. She was a witch after all, a Manchester witch, from a powerful coven of good witches and wizards. Since the age of five, she'd come into her powers. But that wasn't surprising to her family since she was born with magical eyes—one blue and one green.

The enchanted forest was nestled between five properties owned by five different families. Most people didn't know that they were all connected to one another by different paths through the forest which formed a pentagram. A bird's eye view of the forest revealed a pentagram within the circular forest, or so the legend told.

Pentagrams were often found in the Manchester family's *Book of Spells*. Many spells called for drawing pentagrams within the magic circle before chanting magical words to cast a spell. It was no coincidence that Manchester Manor bordered the enchanted forest at the northern point of the pentagram.

Dance wasn't supposed to play in the woods alone. But with dozens of cousins, aunts, and uncles around, she could usually sneak away for an hour or two each day. She'd never encountered another soul in the enchanted forest before, just birds and small animals. And she'd never dared to enter the forest at night because it was just too scary for her overactive imagination.

The trees were enormous, some scaling over three hundred feet. Their foliage provided the darkening canopy of the forest. Today she ventured west towards the sea. Her family had been to the sea on the west coast of the Isle of Skye, but never through the forest. Their horse drawn carriage would take to the shore via the outskirts of the forest.

Walking the path of the north to northwest portion of the pentagram, she searched for the perfect tree to climb. The tall ones offered very few branches on the bottom. She needed a smaller tree that she could climb up, then carefully cross over to a tall tree.

Finally, she found one. Cursing her overbearing mother for making her wear a dress every day, she hiked up her skirt and climbed up onto the first branch. Her arms and legs rapidly ascended the shorter tree. When she reached the top, she did not look down. Instead, she focused on scaling across the long branch to the taller tree whose branches now comingled with those of the smaller one.

After successfully transferring to the taller tree, her fearless body climbed rapidly to the top. Luckily, the tree she'd picked was one of the tallest in the forest, at least the tallest that she'd seen so far. The view from the top of the canopy was breathtaking. She felt like a bird at the top of the forest.

Oh, if only I could fly, she fantasized. Staring west, she found the ocean at the horizon. Just before the ocean on a high cliff stood Castle Garrison. Nearly four hundred years old, the rectangular tower stood five stories tall.

A rustling sound nearby startled her. It sounded

like a large bird flapping its wings. But it wasn't a bird that landed on her tree. It was a boy, a boy with wings!

Terri Talley Venters,
Author of *Carbon Copy, Tin Roof, Silver Lining, Luke's Lithium, Copper Cauldron, Cobalt Cauldron, Calcium Cauldron, Chromium Cauldron, Sulfur Springs, Europium Gem Mine, Noah's Nickel, Manganese Magic, Platinum Princess, Plutonium Princess, Iron Curtains, Body Of Gold & Elements of Mystery*

Terri received her Bachelor's degree in Accounting, and Master's degree in Taxation from the University of Florida. She is a licensed CPA and a Second Degree Black Belt in Taekwondo. She lives on The St. Johns River in Florida, with her husband, Garrison, and their two sons.

Terri is currently writing *Elements Of Mystery* which is a collection of 118 short stories titled after each element in the Periodic Table. For more information about Terri's books, please visit www.ElementsOfMystery.com.

Terri is the daughter of Leslie S. Talley, author of *Make Old Bones, Bred In The Bone, The Closer The Bone & The Bonnie, Bonnie Bone* which are also available at amazon, Barnes & Noble, Smash Words, Kobo & iBooks.

Made in the USA
Columbia, SC
22 June 2023

18628694R10075